The Certain Hour

James Branch Cabell

Contents

THE CERTAIN HOUR

BY

James Branch Cabell

"Criticism, whatever may be its
pretensions, never does more than to
define the impression which is made upon
it at a certain moment by a work wherein
the writer himself noted the impression
of the world which he received at a
certain hour."

NEW YORK
ROBERT M. McBRIDE & COMPANY
1916

TO
ROBERT GAMBLE CABELL II

In Dedication of The Certain Hour

Sad hours and glad hours, and all hours, pass over;
One thing unshaken stays:
Life, that hath Death for spouse, hath Chance for lover;
Whereby decays

Each thing save one thing:--mid this strife diurnal
Of hourly change begot,
Love that is God-born, bides as God eternal,
And changes not;--

Nor means a tinseled dream pursuing lovers
Find altered by-and-bye,
When, with possession, time anon discovers
Trapped dreams must die,--

For he that visions God, of mankind gathers
One manlike trait alone,
And reverently imputes to Him a father's
Love for his son.

BALLAD OF THE DOUBLE-SOUL

"Les Dieux, qui trop aiment ses faceties cruelles"--PAUL VERVILLE.

In the beginning the Gods made man, and fashioned the sky and the sea,
And the earth's fair face for man's dwelling-place, and
this was the Gods' decree:--

"Lo, We have given to man five wits: he discerneth folly and sin;
He is swift to deride all the world outside, and blind
to the world within:

"So that man may make sport and amuse Us, in battling
for phrases or pelf,
Now that each may know what forebodeth woe to his
neighbor, and not to himself."

Yet some have the Gods forgotten,--or is it that subtler mirth
The Gods extort of a certain sort of folk that cumber the earth?

For this is the song of the double-soul, distortedly two in one,--
Of the wearied eyes that still behold the fruit ere the seed be sown,
And derive affright for the nearing night from the light
of the noontide sun.

For one that with hope in the morning set forth, and knew never a fear,

They have linked with another whom omens bother; and
he whispers in one's ear.

And one is fain to be climbing where only angels have trod,
But is fettered and tied to another's side who fears that
it might look odd.

And one would worship a woman whom all perfections dower,
But the other smiles at transparent wiles; and he quotes
from Schopenhauer.

Thus two by two we wrangle and blunder about the earth,
And that body we share we may not spare; but the Gods
have need of mirth.

So this is the song of the double-soul, distortedly two in one.--
Of the wearied eyes that still behold the fruit ere the seed be sown,
And derive affright for the nearing night from the light
of the noontide sun.

AUCTORIAL INDUCTION

These questions, so long as they remain with the Muses, may very well be unaccompanied with severity, for where there is no other end of contemplation and inquiry but that of pastime alone, the understanding is not oppressed; but after the Muses have given over their riddles to Sphinx,--that is, to practise, which urges and impels to action, choice and determination,--then it is that they become torturing, severe and trying."

> From the dawn of the day to the dusk he toiled,
> Shaping fanciful playthings, with tireless hands,--
> Useless trumpery toys; and, with vaulting heart,
> Gave them unto all peoples, who mocked at him,
> Trampled on them, and soiled them, and went their way.
>
> Then he toiled from the morn to the dusk again,
> Gave his gimcracks to peoples who mocked at him,
> Trampled on them, deriding, and went their way.
>
> Thus he labors, and loudly they jeer at him;--
> That is, when they remember he still exists.
>
> *Who*, you ask, *is this fellow*?--What matter names?
> He is only a scribbler who is content.

FELIX KENNASTON.--The Toy-Maker.

AUCTORIAL INDUCTION

WHICH (AFTER SOME BRIEF DISCOURSE OF FIRES AND FRYING-PANS) ELUCIDATES THE INEXPEDIENCY OF PUBLISHING THIS BOOK, AS WELL AS THE NECESSITY OF WRITING IT: AND THENCE PASSES TO A MODEST DEFENSE OF MORE VITAL THEMES.

The desire to write perfectly of beautiful happenings is, as the saying runs, old as the hills--and as immortal. Questionless, there was many a serviceable brick wasted in Nineveh because finicky persons must needs be deleting here and there a phrase in favor of its cuneatic synonym; and it is not improbable that when the outworn sun expires in clinkers its final ray will gild such zealots tinkering with their "style." Some few there must be in every age and every land of whom life claims nothing very insistently save that they write perfectly of beautiful happenings.

Yet, that the work of a man of letters is almost always a congenial product of his day and environment, is a contention as lacking in novelty as it is in the need of any upholding here. Nor is the rationality of that axiom far to seek; for a man of genuine literary genius, since he possesses a temperament whose susceptibilities are of wider area than those of any other, is inevitably of all people the one most variously affected by his surroundings. And it is he, in consequence, who of all people most faithfully and compactly exhibits the impress of his times and his times' tendencies, not merely in his writings--where it conceivably might be just predetermined affectation--but in his personality.

Such being the assumption upon which this volume is builded, it appears only equitable for the architect frankly to indicate his cornerstone. Hereinafter you have an attempt to depict a special temperament--one in essence "literary"--as very variously molded by diverse eras and as responding in proportion with its ability to the demands of a certain hour.

In proportion with its ability, be it repeated, since its ability is singularly hampered. For, apart from any ticklish temporal considerations, be it remembered, life is always claiming of this temperament's possessor that he write perfectly of beautiful happenings.

To disregard this vital longing, and flatly to stifle the innate striving toward artistic creation, is to become (as with Wycherley and Sheridan) a man who waives, however laughingly, his sole apology for existence. The proceeding is paltry enough, in all conscience; and yet, upon the other side, there is much positive danger in giving to the instinct a loose rein. For in that event the familiar circumstances of sedate and wholesome living cannot but seem, like paintings viewed too near, to lose in gusto and winsomeness. Desire, perhaps a craving hunger, awakens for the impossible. No emotion, whatever be its sincerity, is endured without a side-glance toward its capabilities for being written about. The world, in short, inclines to appear an ill-lit mine, wherein one quarries gingerly amidst an abiding loneliness (as with Pope and Ufford and Sire Raimbaut)--and wherein one very often is allured into unsavory alleys (as with Herrick and Alessandro de Medici)--in search of that raw material which loving labor will transshape into comeliness.

Such, if it be allowed to shift the metaphor, are the treacherous by-paths of that admirably policed highway whereon the well-groomed and well-bitted Pegasi of Vanderhoffen and Charteris (in his later manner) trot stolidly and safely toward oblivion. And the result of wandering afield is of necessity a tragedy, in that the deviator's life, if not as an artist's quite certainly as a human being's, must in the outcome be adjudged a failure.

Hereinafter, then, you have an attempt to depict a special temperament--one in essence "literary"--as very variously molded by diverse eras and as responding in proportion with its ability to the demands of a certain hour.

II

And this much said, it is permissible to hope, at least, that here and there some reader may be found not wholly blind to this book's goal, whatever be his opinion as to this book's success in reaching it. Yet many honest souls there be among us average-novel-readers in whose eyes this volume must rest content to figure as a collection of short stories having naught in common beyond the feature that each deals with the ***affaires du coeur*** of a poet.

Such must always be the book's interpretation by mental indolence. The fact is incontestable; and this fact in itself may be taken as sufficient to establish the inexpediency of publishing *The Certain Hour*. For that "people will not buy a volume of short stories" is notorious to all publishers. To offset the axiom there are no doubt incongruous phenomena--ranging from the continued popularity of the Bible to the present general esteem of Mr. Kipling, and embracing the rather unaccountable vogue of "O. Henry";--but, none the less, the superstition has its force.

Here intervenes the multifariousness of man, pointed out somewhere by Mr. Gilbert Chesterton, which enables the individual to be at once a vegetarian, a golfer, a vestryman, a blond, a mammal, a Democrat, and an immortal spirit. As a rational person, one may debonairly consider *The Certain Hour* possesses as large license to look like a volume of short stories as, say, a backgammon-board has to its customary guise of a two-volume history; but as an average-novel-reader, one must vote otherwise. As an average-novel-reader, one must condemn the very book which, as a seasoned scribbler, one was moved to write through long consideration of the drama already suggested--that immemorial drama of the desire to write perfectly of beautiful happenings, and the obscure martyrdom to which this desire solicits its possessor.

Now, clearly, the struggle of a special temperament with a fixed force does not forthwith begin another story when the locale of combat shifts. The case is, rather, as when--with certainly an intervening change of apparel--Pompey fights Caesar at both Dyrrachium and Pharsalus, or as when General Grant successively encounters General Lee at the Wilderness, Spottsylvania, Cold Harbor and Appomattox. The combatants remain unchanged, the question at issue is the same, the tragedy has continuity. And even so, from the time of Sire Raimbaut to that of John Charteris has a special temperament heart-hungrily confronted an ageless problem: at what cost now, in this fleet hour of my vigor, may one write perfectly of beautiful happenings?

Thus logic urges, with pathetic futility, inasmuch as we average-novel-readers are profoundly indifferent to both logic and good writing. And always the fact remains that to the mentally indolent this book may well seem a volume of disconnected short stories. All of us being more or less mentally indolent, this possibility constitutes a dire fault.

Three other damning objections will readily obtrude themselves: *The Certain*

Hour deals with past epochs--beginning before the introduction of dinner-forks, and ending at that remote quaint period when people used to waltz and two-step-- dead eras in which we average-novel-readers are not interested; *The Certain Hour* assumes an appreciable amount of culture and information on its purchaser's part, which we average-novel-readers either lack or, else, are unaccustomed to employ in connection with reading for pastime; and--in our eyes the crowning misdemeanor--The Certain Hour is not "vital."

Having thus candidly confessed these faults committed as the writer of this book, it is still possible in human multifariousness to consider their enormity, not merely in this book, but in fictional reading-matter at large, as viewed by an average-novel-reader--by a representative of that potent class whose preferences dictate the nature and main trend of modern American literature. And to do this, it may be, throws no unsalutary sidelight upon the still-existent problem: at what cost, now, may one attempt to write perfectly of beautiful happenings?

III

Indisputably the most striking defect of this modern American literature is the fact that the production of anything at all resembling literature is scarcely anywhere apparent. Innumerable printing-presses, instead, are turning out a vast quantity of reading-matter, the candidly recognized purpose of which is to kill time, and which- -it has been asserted, though perhaps too sweepingly--ought not to be vended over book-counters, but rather in drugstores along with the other narcotics.

It is begging the question to protest that the class of people who a generation ago read nothing now at least read novels, and to regard this as a change for the better. By similar logic it would be more wholesome to breakfast off laudanum than to omit the meal entirely. The nineteenth century, in fact, by making education popular, has produced in America the curious spectacle of a reading-public with essentially nonliterary tastes. Formerly, better books were published, because they were intended for persons who turned to reading through a natural bent of mind; whereas the modern American novel of commerce is addressed to us average people who read, when we read at all, in violation of every innate instinct.

Such grounds as yet exist for hopefulness on the part of those who cordially care for **belles lettres** are to be found elsewhere than in the crowded market-places of fiction, where genuine intelligence panders on all sides to ignorance and indolence. The phrase may seem to have no very civil ring; but reflection will assure the fair-minded that two indispensable requisites nowadays of a pecuniarily successful novel are, really, that it make no demand upon the reader's imagination, and that it rigorously refrain from assuming its reader to possess any particular information on any subject whatever. The author who writes over the head of the public is the most dangerous enemy of his publisher--and the most insidious as well, because so many publishers are in private life interested in literary matters, and would readily permit this personal foible to influence the exercise of their vocation were it possible to do so upon the preferable side of bankruptcy.

But publishers, among innumerable other conditions, must weigh the fact that no novel which does not deal with modern times is ever really popular among the serious-minded. It is difficult to imagine a tale whose action developed under the rule of the Caesars or the Merovingians being treated as more than a literary **hors d'oeuvre**. We purchasers of "vital" novels know nothing about the period, beyond a hazy association of it with the restrictions of the schoolroom; our sluggish imaginations instinctively rebel against the exertion of forming any notion of such a period; and all the human nature that exists even in serious-minded persons is stirred up to resentment against the book's author for presuming to know more than a potential patron. The book, in fine, simply irritates the serious-minded person; and she--for it is only women who willingly brave the terrors of department-stores, where most of our new books are bought nowadays--quite naturally puts it aside in favor of some keen and daring study of American life that is warranted to grip the reader. So, modernity of scene is everywhere necessitated as an essential qualification for a book's discussion at the literary evenings of the local woman's club; and modernity of scene, of course, is almost always fatal to the permanent worth of fictitious narrative.

It may seem banal here to recall the truism that first-class art never reproduces its surroundings; but such banality is often justified by our human proneness to shuffle over the fact that many truisms are true. And this one is pre-eminently indisputable: that what mankind has generally agreed to accept as first-class art in any of the varied forms of fictitious narrative has never been a truthful reproduction of the artist's era. Indeed, in the higher walks of fiction art has never reproduced anything, but has always dealt with the facts and laws of life as so much crude material which must be transmuted into comeliness. When Shakespeare pronounced his celebrated dictum about art's holding the mirror up to nature, he was no doubt alluding to the circumstance that a mirror reverses everything which it reflects.

Nourishment for much wildish speculation, in fact, can be got by considering what the world's literature would be, had its authors restricted themselves, as do we Americans so sedulously--and unavoidably--to writing of contemporaneous happenings. In fiction-making no author of the first class since Homer's infancy has ever in his happier efforts concerned himself at all with the great "problems" of his particular day; and among geniuses of the second rank you will find such ephemeralities adroitly utilized only when they are distorted into enduring parodies of their actual selves by the broad humor of a Dickens or the colossal fantasy of a Balzac. In such cases as the latter two writers, however, we have an otherwise competent artist handicapped by a personality so marked that, whatever he may nominally write about, the result is, above all else, an exposure of the writer's idiosyncrasies. Then, too, the laws of any locale wherein Mr. Pickwick achieves a competence in business, or of a society wherein Vautrin becomes chief of police, are upon the face of it extra-mundane. It suffices that, as a general rule, in fiction-making the true artist finds an ample, if restricted, field wherein the proper functions of the preacher, or the ventriloquist, or the photographer, or of the public prosecutor, are exercised with equal lack of grace.

Besides, in dealing with contemporary life a novelist is goaded into too many pusillanimous concessions to plausibility. He no longer moves with the gait of omnipotence. It was very different in the palmy days when Dumas was free to play at ducks and drakes with history, and Victor Hugo to reconstruct the whole system of English government, and Scott to compel the sun to set in the east, whenever such minor changes caused to flow more smoothly the progress of the tale these giants had in hand. These freedoms are not tolerated in American noveldom, and only a few futile "high-brows" sigh in vain for Thackeray's "happy harmless Fableland, where these things are." The majority of us are deep in "vital" novels. Nor is the reason far to seek.

IV

One hears a great deal nowadays concerning "vital" books. Their authors have been widely praised on very various grounds. Oddly enough, however, the writers of these books have rarely been commended for the really praiseworthy charity evinced therein toward that large long-suffering class loosely describable as the average-novel-reader.

Yet, in connection with this fact, it is worthy of more than passing note that no great while ago the ***New York Times'*** carefully selected committee, in picking out the hundred best books published during a particular year, declared as to novels--"a 'best' book, in our opinion, is one that raises an important question, or recurs to a vital theme and pronounces upon it what in some sense is a last word." Now this definition is not likely ever to receive more praise than it deserves. Cavilers may, of course, complain that actually to write the last word on any subject is a feat reserved for the Recording Angel's unique performance on judgment Day. Even setting that objection aside, it is undeniable that no work of fiction published of late in America corresponds quite so accurately to the terms of this definition as do the multiplication tables. Yet the multiplication tables are not without their claims to applause as examples of straightforward narrative. It is, also, at least permissible to consider that therein the numeral five, say, where it figures as protagonist, unfolds under the stress of its varying adventures as opulent a development of real human nature as does, through similar ups-and-downs, the Reverend John Hodder in ***The Inside of the Cup***. It is equally allowable to find the less simple evolution of the digit seven more sympathetic, upon the whole, than those of Undine Spragg in ***The Custom of the Country***. But, even so, this definition of what may now, authoritatively, be ranked as a "best novel" is an honest and noteworthy severance from misleading literary associations such as have too long befogged our notions about reading-matter. It points with emphasis toward the altruistic obligations of tale-tellers to be "vital."

For we average-novel-readers--we average people, in a word--are now, as always, rather pathetically hungry for "vital" themes, such themes as appeal directly to our everyday observation and prejudices. Did the decision rest with us all novelists would be put under bond to confine themselves forevermore to themes like these. As touches the appeal to everyday observation, it is an old story, at least co-eval with Mr. Crummles' not uncelebrated pumps and tubs, if not with the grapes of Zeuxis, how unfailingly in art we delight to recognize the familiar. A novel whose scene of action is explicit will always interest the people of that locality, whatever the book's other pretensions to consideration. Given simultaneously a photograph of Murillo's rendering of *The Virgin Crowned Queen of Heaven* and a photograph of a governor's installation in our State capital, there is no one of us but will quite naturally look at the latter first, in order to see if in it some familiar countenance be recognizable. And thus, upon a larger scale, the twentieth century is, pre-eminently, interested in the twentieth century.

It is all very well to describe our average-novel-readers' dislike of Romanticism as "the rage of Caliban not seeing his own face in a glass." It is even within the scope of human dunderheadedness again to point out here that the supreme artists in literature have precisely this in common, and this alone, that in their masterworks they have avoided the "vital" themes of their day with such circumspection as lesser folk reserve for the smallpox. The answer, of course, in either case, is that the "vital" novel, the novel which peculiarly appeals to us average-novel-readers, has nothing to do with literature. There is between these two no more intelligent connection than links the paint Mr. Sargent puts on canvas and the paint Mr. Dockstader puts on his face.

Literature is made up of the re-readable books, the books which it is possible--for the people so constituted as to care for that sort of thing--to read again and yet again with pleasure. Therefore, in literature a book's subject is of astonishingly minor importance, and its style nearly everything: whereas in books intended to be read for pastime, and forthwith to be consigned at random to the wastebasket or to the inmates of some charitable institute, the theme is of paramount importance, and ought to be a serious one. The modern novelist owes it to his public to select a "vital" theme which in itself will fix the reader's attention by reason of its familiarity in the reader's everyday life.

Thus, a lady with whose more candid opinions the writer of this is more frequently favored nowadays than of old, formerly confessed to having only one set rule when it came to investment in new reading-matter--always to buy the Williamsons' last book. Her reason was the perfectly sensible one that the Williamsons' plots used invariably to pivot upon motor-trips, and she is an ardent automobilist. Since, as of late, the Williamsons have seen fit to exercise their typewriter upon other topics, they have as a matter of course lost her patronage.

This principle of selection, when you come to appraise it sanely, is the sole intelligent method of dealing with reading-matter. It seems here expedient again to state the peculiar problem that we average-novel-readers have of necessity set the modern novelist--namely, that his books must in the main appeal to people who read for pastime, to people who read books only under protest and only when they have no other employment for that particular half-hour.

Now, reading for pastime is immensely simplified when the book's theme is some familiar matter of the reader's workaday life, because at outset the reader is spared considerable mental effort. The motorist above referred to, and indeed any average-novel-reader, can without exertion conceive of the Williamsons' people in their automobiles. Contrariwise, were these fictitious characters embarked in palankeens or droshkies or jinrikishas, more or less intellectual exercise would be necessitated on the reader's part to form a notion of the conveyance. And we average-novel-readers do not open a book with the intention of making a mental effort. The author has no right to expect of us an act so unhabitual, we very poignantly feel. Our prejudices he is freely chartered to stir up--if, lucky rogue, he can!--but he ought with deliberation to recognize that it is precisely in order to avoid mental effort that we purchase, or borrow, his book, and afterward discuss it.

Hence arises our heartfelt gratitude toward such novels as deal with "vital" themes, with the questions we average-novel-readers confront or make talk about in those happier hours of our existence wherein we are not reduced to reading. Thus, a tale, for example, dealing either with "feminism" or "white slavery" as the handiest makeshift of spinsterdom--or with the divorce habit and plutocratic iniquity in general, or with the probable benefits of converting clergymen to Christianity, or with how much more than she knows a desirable mother will tell her children--finds the book's tentative explorer, just now, amply equipped with prejudices, whether acquired by second thought or second hand, concerning the book's topic. As endurability goes, reading the book rises forthwith almost to the level of an afternoon-call where there is gossip about the neighbors and Germany's future. We average-novel-readers may not, in either case, agree with the opinions advanced; but at least our prejudices are aroused, and we are interested.

And these "vital" themes awake our prejudices at the cost of a minimum--if not always, as when Miss Corelli guides us, with a positively negligible--tasking of our mental faculties. For such exemption we average-novel-readers cannot but be properly grateful. Nay, more than this: provided the novelist contrive to rouse our prejudices, it matters with us not at all whether afterward they be soothed or harrowed. To implicate our prejudices somehow, to raise in us a partizanship in the tale's progress, is our sole request. Whether this consummation be brought about through an arraignment of some social condition which we personally either advocate or reprehend--the attitude weighs little--or whether this interest be purchased with placidly driveling preachments of generally "uplifting" tendencies--vaguely titillating that vague intention which exists in us all of becoming immaculate as soon as it is perfectly convenient--the personal prejudices of us average-novel-readers are not lightly lulled again to sleep.

In fact, the jealousy of any human prejudice against hinted encroachment may safely be depended upon to spur us through an astonishing number of pages--for all that it has of late been complained among us, with some show of extenuation, that our original intent in beginning certain of the recent "vital" novels was to kill time, rather than eternity. And so, we average-novel-readers plod on jealously to the end, whether we advance (to cite examples already somewhat of yesterday) under the leadership of Mr. Upton Sinclair aspersing the integrity of modern sausages and millionaires, or of Mr. Hall Caine saying about Roman Catholics what ordinary people would hesitate to impute to their relatives by marriage--or whether we be more suavely allured onward by Mrs. Florence Barclay, or Mr. Sydnor Harrison, with ingenuous indorsements of the New Testament and the inherent womanliness of women. The "vital" theme, then, let it be repeated, has two inestimable advantages which should commend it to all novelists: first, it spares us average-novel-readers any preliminary orientation, and thereby mitigates the mental exertion of reading; and secondly, it appeals to our prejudices, which we naturally prefer to exercise, and are accustomed to exercise, rather than our mental or idealistic faculties. The novelist who conscientiously bears these two facts in mind is reasonably sure of his reward, not merely in pecuniary form, but in those higher fields wherein he harvests his chosen public's honest gratitude and affection.

For we average-novel-readers are quite frequently reduced by circumstances to self-entrustment to the resources of the novelist, as to those of the dentist. Our latter-day conditions, as we cannot but recognize, necessitate the employment of both artists upon occasion. And with both, we average-novel-readers, we average people, are most grateful when they make the process of resorting to them as easy and unirritating as may be possible.

V

So much for the plea of us average-novel-readers; and our plea, we think, is rational. We are "in the market" for a specified article; and human ingenuity, co-operating with human nature, will inevitably insure the manufacture of that article as long as any general demand for it endures.

Meanwhile, it is small cause for grief that the purchaser of American novels prefers Central Park to any "wood near Athens," and is more at home in the Tenderloin than in Camelot. People whose tastes happen to be literary are entirely too prone to too much long-faced prattle about literature, which, when all is said, is never a controlling factor in anybody's life. The automobile and the telephone, the accomplishments of Mr. Edison and Mr. Burbank, and it would be permissible to add of Mr. Rockefeller, influence nowadays, in one fashion or another, every moment of every living American's existence; whereas had America produced, instead, a second Milton or a Dante, it would at most have caused a few of us to spend a few spare evenings rather differently. Besides, we know--even we average-novel-readers--that America is in fact producing her enduring literature day by day, although, as rarely fails to be the case, those who are contemporaneous with the makers of this literature cannot with any certainty point them out. To voice a hoary truism, time alone is the test of "vitality." In our present flood of books, as in any other flood, it is the froth and scum which shows most prominently. And the possession of "vitality," here as elsewhere, postulates that its possessor must ultimately perish.

Nay, by the time these printed pages are first read as printed pages, allusion to those modern authors whom these pages cite--the pre-eminent literary personages of that hour wherein these pages were written--will inevitably have come to savor somewhat of antiquity: so that sundry references herein to the "vital" books now most in vogue will rouse much that vague shrugging recollection as wakens, say, at a mention of **Dorothy Vernon** or **Three Weeks** or **Beverly of Graustark**. And while at first glance it might seem expedient--in revising the last proof-sheets of these pages--somewhat to "freshen them up" by substituting, for the books herein referred to, the "vital" and more widely talked-of novels of the summer of 1916, the task would be but wasted labor; since even these fascinating chronicles, one comprehends forlornly, must needs be equally obsolete by the time these proof-sheets have been made into a volume. With malice aforethought, therefore, the books and authors named herein stay those which all of three years back our reviewers and advertising pages, with perfect gravity, acclaimed as of enduring importance. For the quaintness of that opinion, nowadays, may profitably round the moral that there is really nothing whereto one may fittingly compare a successful contribution to "vital" reading-matter, as touches evanescence.

And this is as it should be. ***Tout passe.--L'art robust seul a l'eternite***, precisely as Gautier points out, with bracing common-sense; and it is excellent thus to comprehend that to-day, as always, only through exercise of the auctorial virtues of distinction and clarity, of beauty and symmetry, of tenderness and truth and urbanity, may a man in reason attempt to insure his books against oblivion's voracity.

Yet the desire to write perfectly of beautiful happenings is, as the saying runs, old as the hills--and as immortal. Questionless, there was many a serviceable brick wasted in Nineveh because finicky persons must needs be deleting here and there a phrase in favor of its cuneatic synonym; and it is not improbable that when the outworn sun expires in clinkers its final ray will gild such zealots tinkering with their "style." This, then, is the conclusion of the whole matter. Some few there must be in every age and every land of whom life claims nothing very insistently save that they write perfectly of beautiful happenings. And even we average-novel-readers know it is such folk who are to-day making in America that portion of our literature which may hope for permanency.

Dumbarton Grange
1914-1916

BELHS CAVALIERS

For this RAIMBAUT DE VAQUIERAS lived at a time when prolonged habits of extra-mundane contemplation, combined with the decay of real knowledge, were apt to volatilize the thoughts and aspirations of the best and wisest into dreamy unrealities, and to lend a false air of mysticism to love. . . . It is as if the intellect and the will had become used to moving paralytically among visions, dreams, and mystic terrors, weighed down with torpor."

Fair friend, since that hour I took leave of thee
I have not slept nor stirred from off my knee,
But prayed alway to God, S. Mary's Son,
To give me back my true companion;
    And soon it will be Dawn.

Fair friend, at parting, thy behest to me
Was that all sloth I should eschew and flee,
And keep good Watch until the Night was done:
Now must my Song and Service pass for none?
    For soon it will be Dawn.

RAIMBAUT DE VAQUIERAS.--Aubade, from F. York Powell's version.

BELHS CAVALIERS

You may read elsewhere of the long feud that was between Guillaume de Baux, afterward Prince of Orange, and his kinsman Raimbaut de Vaquieras. They were not reconciled until their youth was dead. Then, when Messire Raimbaut returned from battling against the Turks and the Bulgarians, in the 1,210th year from man's salvation, the Archbishop of Rheims made peace between the two cousins; and, attended by Makrisi, a converted Saracen who had followed the knight's fortunes for well nigh a quarter of a century, the Sire de Vaquieras rode homeward.

Many slain men were scattered along the highway when he came again into Venaissin, in April, after an absence of thirty years. The crows whom his passing disturbed were too sluggish for long flights and many of them did not heed him at all. Guillaume de Baux was now undisputed master of these parts, although, as this host of mute, hacked and partially devoured witnesses attested, the contest had been dubious for a while: but now Lovain of the Great-Tooth, Prince Guillaume's last competitor, was captured; the forces of Lovain were scattered; and of Lovain's lieutenants only Mahi de Vernoil was unsubdued.

Prince Guillaume laughed a little when he told his kinsman of the posture of affairs, as more loudly did Guillaume's gross son, Sire Philibert. But Madona Biatritz did not laugh. She was the widow of Guillaume's dead brother--Prince Conrat, whom Guillaume succeeded--and it was in her honor that Raimbaut had made those songs which won him eminence as a practitioner of the Gay Science.

Biatritz said, "It is a long while since we two met."

He that had been her lover all his life said, "Yes."

She was no longer the most beautiful of women, no longer his be-hymned Belhs Cavaliers--you may read elsewhere how he came to call her that in all his canzons--but only a fine and gracious stranger. It was uniformly gray, that soft and plentiful hair, where once such gold had flamed as dizzied him to think of even now; there was no crimson in these thinner lips; and candor would have found her eyes less wonderful than those Raimbaut had dreamed of very often among an alien and hostile people. But he lamented nothing, and to him she was as ever Heaven's most splendid miracle.

"Yes," said this old Raimbaut,--"and even to-day we have not reclaimed the Sepulcher as yet. Oh, I doubt if we shall ever win it, now that your brother and my most dear lord is dead." Both thought a while of Boniface de Montferrat, their playmate once, who yesterday was King of Thessalonica and now was so much Macedonian dust.

She said: "This week the Prince sent envoys to my nephew. . . . And so you have come home again----" Color had surged into her time-worn face, and as she thought of things done long ago this woman's eyes were like the eyes of his young Biatritz. She said: "You never married?"

He answered: "No, I have left love alone. For Love prefers to take rather than to give; against a single happy hour he balances a hundred miseries, and he appraises one pleasure to be worth a thousand pangs. Pardieu, let this immortal usurer contrive as may seem well to him, for I desire no more of his bounty or of his penalties."

"No, we wish earnestly for nothing, either good or bad," said Dona Biatritz--"we who have done with loving."

They sat in silence, musing over ancient happenings, and not looking at each other, until the Prince came with his guests, who seemed to laugh too heartily.

Guillaume's frail arm was about his kinsman, and Guillaume chuckled over jests and by-words that had been between the cousins as children. Raimbaut found them no food for laughter now. Guillaume told all of Raimbaut's oath of fealty, and of how these two were friends and their unnatural feud was forgotten. "For we grow old,--eh, maker of songs?" he said; "and it is time we made our peace with Heaven, since we are not long for this world."

"Yes," said the knight; "oh yes, we both grow old." He thought of another April evening, so long ago, when this Guillaume de Baux had stabbed him in a hedged field near Calais, and had left him under a hawthorn bush for dead; and Raimbaut wondered that there was no anger in his heart. "We are friends now," he said. Biatritz, whom these two had loved, and whose vanished beauty had been the spur of their long enmity, sat close to them, and hardly seemed to listen.

Thus the evening passed and every one was merry, because the Prince had overcome Lovain of the Great-Tooth, and was to punish the upstart on the morrow.

But Raimbaut de Vaquieras, a spent fellow, a derelict, barren of aim now that the Holy Wars were over, sat in this unfamiliar place--where when he was young he had laughed as a cock crows!--and thought how at the last he had crept home to die as a dependent on his cousin's bounty.

Thus the evening passed, and at its end Makrisi followed the troubadour to his regranted fief of Vaquieras. This was a chill and brilliant night, swayed by a frozen moon so powerful that no stars showed in the unclouded heavens, and everywhere the bogs were curdled with thin ice. An obdurate wind swept like a knife-blade across a world which even in its spring seemed very old.

"This night is bleak and evil," Makrisi said. He rode a coffin's length behind his master. "It is like Prince Guillaume, I think. What man will sorrow when dawn comes?"

Raimbaut de Vaquieras replied: "Always dawn comes at last, Makrisi."

"It comes the more quickly, messire, when it is prompted."

The troubadour only smiled at words which seemed so meaningless. He did not smile when later in the night Makrisi brought Mahi de Vernoil, disguised as a mendicant friar. This outlaw pleaded with Sire Raimbaut to head the tatters of Lovain's army, and showed Raimbaut how easy it would be to wrest Venaissin from Prince Guillaume. "We cannot save Lovain," de Vemoil said, "for Guillaume has him fast. But Venaissin is very proud of you, my tres beau sire. Ho, maker of world-famous songs! stout champion of the faith! my men and I will now make you Prince of Orange in place of the fiend who rules us. You may then at your convenience wed Madona Biatritz, that most amiable lady whom you have loved so long. And by the Cross! you may do this before the week is out."

The old knight answered: "It is true that I have always served Madona Biatritz, who is of matchless worth. I might not, therefore, presume to call myself any longer her servant were my honor stained in any particular. Oh no, Messire de Vernoil, an oath is an oath. I have this day sworn fealty to Guillaume de Baux."

Then after other talk Raimbaut dismissed the fierce-eyed little man. The freebooter growled curses as he went. On a sudden he whistled, like a person considering, and he began to chuckle.

Raimbaut said, more lately: "Zoraida left no wholesome legacy in you, Makrisi." This Zoraida was a woman the knight had known in Constantinople--a comely outlander who had killed herself because of Sire Raimbaut's highflown avoidance of all womankind except the mistress of his youth.

"Nay, save only in loving you too well, messire, was Zoraida a wise woman, notably. . . . But this is outworn talk, the prattle of Cain's babyhood. As matters were, you did not love Zoraida. So Zoraida died. Such is the custom in my country."

"You trouble me, Makrisi. Your eyes are like blown coals. . . . Yet you have served me long and faithfully. You know that mine was ever the vocation of dealing honorably in battle among emperors, and of spreading broadcast the rumor of my valor, and of achieving good by my sword's labors. I have lived by warfare. Long, long ago, since I derived no benefit from love, I cried farewell to it."

"Ay," said Makrisi. "Love makes a demi-god of all--just for an hour. Such hours as follow we devote to the concoction of sleeping-draughts." He laughed, and very harshly.

And Raimbaut did not sleep that night because this life of ours seemed such a piece of tangle-work as he had not the skill to unravel. So he devoted the wakeful hours to composition of a planh, lamenting vanished youth and that Biatritz whom the years had stolen.

Then on the ensuing morning, after some talk about the new campaign, Prince Guillaume de Baux leaned back in his high chair and said, abruptly:

"In perfect candor, you puzzle your liege-lord. For you loathe me and you still worship my sister-in-law, an unattainable princess. In these two particulars you display such wisdom as would inevitably prompt you to make an end of me. Yet, what the devil! you, the time-battered vagabond, decline happiness and a kingdom to boot because of yesterday's mummery in the cathedral! because of a mere promise given! Yes, I have my spies in every rat-hole. I am aware that my barons hate me, and hate Philibert almost as bitterly,--and that, in fine, a majority of my barons would prefer to see you Prince in my unstable place, on account of your praiseworthy molestations of heathenry. Oh, yes, I understand my barons perfectly. I flatter myself I understand everybody in Venaissin save you."

Raimbaut answered: "You and I are not alike."

"No, praise each and every Saint!" said the Prince of Orange, heartily. "And yet, I am not sure----" He rose, for his sight had failed him so that he could not distinctly see you except when he spoke with head thrown back, as though he looked at you over a wall. "For instance, do you understand that I hold Biatritz here as a prisoner, because her dower-lands are necessary to me, and that I intend to marry her as soon as Pope Innocent grants me a dispensation?"

"All Venaissin knows that. Yes, you have always gained everything which you desired in this world, Guillaume. Yet it was at a price, I think."

"I am no haggler. . . . But you have never comprehended me, not even in the old days when we loved each other. For instance, do you understand--slave of a spoken word!--what it must mean to me to know that at this hour to-morrow there will be alive in Venaissin no person whom I hate?"

Messire de Vaquieras reflected. His was never a rapid mind. "Why, no, I do not know anything about hatred," he said, at last. "I think I never hated any person."

Guillaume de Baux gave a half-frantic gesture. "Now, Heaven send you troubadours a clearer understanding of what sort of world we live in----!" He broke off short and growled, "And yet--sometimes I envy you, Raimbaut!"

They rode then into the Square of St. Michel to witness the death of Lovain. Guillaume took with him his two new mistresses and all his by-blows, each magnificently clothed, as if they rode to a festival. Afterward, before the doors of Lovain's burning house, a rope was fastened under Lovain's armpits, and he was gently lowered into a pot of boiling oil. His feet cooked first, and then the flesh of his legs, and so on upward, while Lovain screamed. Guillaume in a loose robe of green powdered with innumerable silver crescents, sat watching, under a canopy woven very long ago in Tarshish, and cunningly embroidered with the figures of peacocks and apes and men with eagles' heads. His hands caressed each other meditatively.

It was on the afternoon of this day, the last of April, that Sire Raimbaut came upon Madona Biatritz about a strange employment in the Ladies' Court. There was then a well in the midst of this enclosure, with a granite ledge around it carven with lilies; and upon this she leaned, looking down into the water. In her lap was a rope of pearls, which one by one she unthreaded and dropped into the well.

Clear and warm the weather was. Without, forests were quickening, branch by branch, as though a green flame smoldered from one bough to another. Violets peeped about the roots of trees, and all the world was young again. But here was only stone beneath their feet; and about them showed the high walls and the lead-sheathed towers and the parapets and the sunk windows of Guillaume's chateau. There was no color anywhere save gray; and Raimbaut and Biatritz were aging people now. It seemed to him that they were the wraiths of those persons who had loved each other at Montferrat; and that the walls about them and the leaden devils who grinned from every waterspout and all those dark and narrow windows were only part of some magic picture, such as a sorceress may momentarily summon out of smoke-wreaths, as he had seen Zoraida do very long ago.

This woman might have been a wraith in verity, for she was clothed throughout in white, save for the ponderous gold girdle about her middle. A white gorget framed the face which was so pinched and shrewd and strange; and she peered into the well, smiling craftily.

"I was thinking death was like this well," said Biatritz, without any cessation of her singular employment--"so dark that we may see nothing clearly save one faint gleam which shows us, or which seems to show us, where rest is. Yes, yes, this is that chaplet which you won in the tournament at Montferrat when we were young. Pearls are the symbol of tears, we read. But we had no time for reading then, no time for anything except to be quite happy. . . . You saw this morning's work. Raimbaut, were Satan to go mad he would be such a fiend as this Guillaume de Baux who is our master!"

"Ay, the man is as cruel as my old opponent, Mourzoufle," Sire Raimbaut answered, with a patient shrug. "It is a great mystery why such persons should win all which they desire of this world. We can but recognize that it is for some sufficient reason." Then he talked with her concerning the aforementioned infamous emperor of the East, against whom the old knight had fought, and of Enrico Dandolo and of King Boniface, dead brother to Madona Biatritz, and of much remote, outlandish adventuring oversea. Of Zoraida he did not speak. And Biatritz, in turn, told him of that one child which she had borne her husband, Prince Conrat--a son who died in infancy; and she spoke of this dead baby, who living would have been their monarch, with a sweet quietude that wrung the old knight's heart.

Thus these spent people sat and talked for a long while, the talk veering anywhither just as chance directed. Blurred gusts of song and laughter would come to them at times from the hall where Guillaume de Baux drank with his courtiers, and these would break the tranquil flow of speech. Then, unvexedly, the gentle voice of the speaker, were it his or hers, would resume.

She said: "They laugh. We are not merry."

"No," he replied; "I am not often merry. There was a time when love and its service kept me in continuous joy, as waters invest a fish. I woke from a high dream. . . . And then, but for the fear of seeming cowardly, I would have extinguished my life as men blow out a candle. Vanity preserved me, sheer vanity!" He shrugged, spreading his hard lean hands. "Belhs Cavaliers, I grudged my enemies the pleasure of seeing me forgetful of valor and noble enterprises. And so, since then, I have served Heaven, in default of you."

"I would not have it otherwise," she said, half as in wonder; "I would not have you be quite sane like other men. And I believe," she added--still with her wise smile--"you have derived a deal of comfort, off and on, from being heart-broken."

He replied gravely: "A man may always, if he will but take the pains, be tolerably content and rise in worth, and yet dispense with love. He has only to guard himself against baseness, and concentrate his powers on doing right. Thus, therefore, when fortune failed me, I persisted in acting to the best of my ability. Though I had lost my lands and my loved lady, I must hold fast to my own worth. Without a lady and without acreage, it was yet in my power to live a cleanly and honorable life; and I did not wish to make two evils out of one."

"Assuredly, I would not have you be quite sane like other men," she repeated. "It would seem that you have somehow blundered through long years, preserving always the ignorance of a child, and the blindness of a child. I cannot understand how this is possible; nor can I keep from smiling at your high-flown notions; and yet,--I envy you, Raimbaut."

Thus the afternoon passed, and the rule of Prince Guillaume was made secure. His supper was worthily appointed, for Guillaume loved color and music and beauty of every kind, and was on this, the day of his triumph, in a prodigal humor. Many lackeys in scarlet brought in the first course, to the sound of exultant drums and pipes, with a blast of trumpets and a waving of banners, so that all hearts were uplifted, and Guillaume jested with harsh laughter.

But Raimbaut de Vaquieras was not mirthful, for he was remembering a boy whom he had known of very long ago. He was swayed by an odd fancy, as the men sat over their wine, and jongleurs sang and performed tricks for their diversion, that this boy, so frank and excellent, as yet existed somewhere; and that the Raimbaut who moved these shriveled hands before him, on the table there, was only a sad dream of what had never been. It troubled him, too, to see how grossly these soldiers ate, for, as a person of refinement, an associate of monarchs, Sire Raimbaut when the dishes were passed picked up his meats between the index- and the middle-finger of his left hand, and esteemed it infamous manners to dip any other fingers into the gravy.

Guillaume had left the Warriors' Hall. Philibert was drunk, and half the men-at-arms were snoring among the rushes, when at the height of their festivity Makrisi came. He plucked his master by the sleeve.

A swarthy, bearded Angevin was singing. His song was one of old Sire Raimbaut's famous canzons in honor of Belhs Cavaliers. The knave was singing blithely:

Pus mos Belhs Cavaliers grazitz
E joys m'es lunhatz e faiditz,
Don no m' venra jamais conortz;
Fer qu'ees mayer l'ira e plus fortz--

The Saracen had said nothing. He showed a jeweled dagger, and the knight arose and followed him out of that uproarious hall. Raimbaut was bitterly perturbed, though he did not know for what reason, as Makrisi led him through dark corridors to the dull-gleaming arras of Prince Guillaume's apartments. In this corridor was an iron lamp swung from the ceiling, and now, as this lamp swayed slightly and burned low, the tiny flame leaped clear of the wick and was extinguished, and darkness rose about them.

Raimbaut said: "What do you want of me? Whose blood is on that knife?"

"Have you forgotten it is Walburga's Eve?" Makrisi said. Raimbaut did not regret he could not see his servant's countenance. "Time was we named it otherwise and praised another woman than a Saxon wench, but let the new name stand. It is Walburga's Eve, that little, little hour of evil! and all over the world surges the full tide of hell's desire, and mischief is a-making now, apace, apace, apace. People moan in their sleep, and many pillows are pricked by needles that have sewed a shroud. Cry **Eman hetan** now, messire! for there are those to-night who find the big cathedrals of your red-roofed Christian towns no more imposing than so many pimples on a butler's chin, because they ride so high, so very high, in this brave moonlight. Full-tide, full-tide!" Makrisi said, and his voice jangled like a bell as he drew aside the curtain so that the old knight saw into the room beyond.

It was a place of many lights, which, when thus suddenly disclosed, blinded him at first. Then Raimbaut perceived Guillaume lying a-sprawl across an oaken chest. The Prince had fallen backward and lay in this posture, glaring at the intruders with horrible eyes which did not move and would not ever move again. His breast was crimson, for some one had stabbed him. A woman stood above the corpse and lighted yet another candle while Raimbaut de Vaquieras waited motionless. A hand meant only to bestow caresses brushed a lock of hair from this woman's eyes while he waited. The movements of this hand were not uncertain, but only quivered somewhat, as a taut wire shivers in the wind, while Raimbaut de Vaquieras waited motionless.

"I must have lights, I must have a host of candles to assure me past any questioning that he is dead. The man is of deep cunning. I think he is not dead even now." Lightly Biatritz touched the Prince's breast. "Strange, that this wicked heart should be so tranquil when there is murder here to make it glad! Nay, very certainly this Guillaume de Baux will rise and laugh in his old fashion before he speaks, and then I shall be afraid. But I am not afraid as yet. I am afraid of nothing save the dark, for one cannot be merry in the dark."

Raimbaut said: "This is Belhs Cavaliers whom I have loved my whole life through. Therefore I do not doubt. Pardieu, I do not even doubt, who know she is of matchless worth."

"Wherein have I done wrong, Raimbaut?" She came to him with fluttering hands. "Why, but look you, the man had laid an ambuscade in the marsh and he meant to kill you there to-night as you rode for Vaquieras. He told me of it, told me how it was for that end alone he lured you into Venaissin----" Again she brushed the hair back from her forehead. "Raimbaut, I spoke of God and knightly honor, and the man laughed. No, I think it was a fiend who sat so long beside the window yonder, whence one may see the marsh. There were no candles in the room. The moonlight was upon his evil face, and I could think of nothing, of nothing that has been since Adam's time, except our youth, Raimbaut. And he smiled fixedly, like a white image, because my misery amused him. Only, when I tried to go to you to warn you, he leaped up stiffly, making a mewing noise. He caught me by the throat so that I could not scream. Then while we struggled in the moonlight your Makrisi came and stabbed him----"

"Nay, I but fetched this knife, messire." Makrisi seemed to love that bloodied knife.

Biatritz proudly said: "The man lies, Raimbaut."

"What need to tell me that, Belhs Cavaliers?"

And the Saracen shrugged. "It is very true I lie," he said. "As among friends, I may confess I killed the Prince. But for the rest, take notice both of you, I mean to lie intrepidly."

Raimbaut remembered how his mother had given each of two lads an apple, and he had clamored for Guillaume's, as children do, and Guillaume had changed with him. It was a trivial happening to remember after fifty years; but Guillaume was dead, and this hacked flesh was Raimbaut's flesh in part, and the thought of Raimbaut would never trouble Guillaume de Baux any more. In addition there was a fire of juniper wood and frankincense upon the hearth, and the room smelt too cloyingly of be-drugging sweetness. Then on the walls were tapestries which depicted Merlin's Dream, so that everywhere recoiling women smiled with bold eyes; and here their wantonness seemed out of place.

"Listen," Makrisi was saying; "listen, for the hour strikes. At last, at last!" he cried, with a shrill whine of malice.

Raimbaut said, dully: "Oh, I do not understand----"

"And yet Zoraida loved you once! loved you as people love where I was born!" The Saracen's voice had altered. His speech was like the rustle of papers. "You did not love Zoraida. And so it came about that upon Walburga's Eve, at midnight, Zoraida hanged herself beside your doorway. Thus we love where I was born. . . . And I, I cut the rope--with my left hand. I had my other arm about that frozen thing which yesterday had been Zoraida, you understand, so that it might not fall. And in the act a tear dropped from that dead woman's cheek and wetted my forehead. Ice is not so cold as was that tear. . . . Ho, that tear did not fall upon my forehead but on my heart, because I loved that dancing-girl, Zoraida, as you do this princess here. I think you will understand," Makrisi said, calmly as one who states a maxim.

The Sire de Vaquieras replied, in the same tone: "I understand. You have contrived my death?"

"Ey, messire, would that be adequate? I could have managed that any hour within the last score of years. Oh no! for I have studied you carefully. Oh no! instead, I have contrived this plight. For the Prince of Orange is manifestly murdered. Who killed him?--why, Madona Biatritz, and none other, for I will swear to it. I, I will swear to it, who saw it done. Afterward both you and I must be questioned upon the rack, as possibly concerned in the affair, and whether innocent or guilty we must die very horribly. Such is the gentle custom of your Christian country when a prince is murdered. That is not the point of the jest, however. For first Sire Philibert will put this woman to the Question by Water, until she confesses her confederates, until she confesses that every baron whom Philibert distrusts was one of them. Oh yes, assuredly they will thrust a hollow cane into the mouth of your Biatritz, and they will pour water a little by a little through this cane, until she confesses what they desire. Ha, Philibert will see to this confession! And through this woman's torment he will rid himself of every dangerous foe he has in Venaissin. You must stand by and wait your turn. You must stand by, in fetters, and see this done--you, you, my master!--you, who love this woman as I loved that dead Zoraida who was not fair enough to please you!"

Raimbaut, trapped, impotent, cried out: "This is not possible----" And for all that, he knew the Saracen to be foretelling the inevitable.

Makrisi went on, quietly: "After the Question men will parade her, naked to the middle, through all Orange, until they reach the Marketplace, where will be four horses. One of these horses they will harness to each arm and leg of your Biatritz. Then they will beat these horses. These will be strong horses. They will each run in a different direction."

This infamy also was certain. Raimbaut foresaw what he must do. He clutched the dagger which Makrisi fondled. "Belhs Cavaliers, this fellow speaks the truth. Look now, the moon is old--is it not strange to know it will outlive us?"

And Biatritz came close to Sire Raimbaut and said: "I understand. If I leave this room alive it will purchase a hideous suffering for my poor body, it will bring about the ruin of many brave and innocent chevaliers. I know. I would perforce confess all that the masked men bade me. I know, for in Prince Conrat's time I have seen persons who had been put to the Question----" She shuddered; and she re-began, without any agitation: "Give me the knife, Raimbaut."

"Pardieu! but I may not obey you for this once," he answered, "since we are informed by those in holy orders that all such as lay violent hands upon themselves must suffer eternally." Then, kneeling, he cried, in an extremity of adoration: "Oh, I have served you all my life. You may not now deny me this last service. And while I talk they dig your grave! O blind men, making the new grave, take heed lest that grave be too narrow, for already my heart is breaking in my body. I have drunk too deep of sorrow. And yet I may not fail you, now that honor and mercy and my love for you demand I kill you before I also die--in such a fashion as this fellow speaks of."

She did not dispute this. How could she when it was an axiom in all Courts of Love that Heaven held dominion in a lover's heart only as an underling of the man's mistress?

And so she said, with a fond smile: "It is your demonstrable privilege. I would not grant it, dear, were my weak hands as clean as yours. Oh, but it is long you have loved me, and it is faithfully you have served Heaven, and my heart too is breaking in my body now that your service ends!"

And he demanded, wearily: "When we were boy and girl together what had we said if any one had told us this would be the end?"

"We would have laughed. It is a long while since those children laughed at Montferrat. . . . Not yet, not yet!" she said. "Ah, pity me, tried champion, for even now I am almost afraid to die."

She leaned against the window yonder, shuddering, staring into the night. Dawn had purged the east of stars. Day was at hand, the day whose noon she might not hope to witness. She noted this incuriously. Then Biatritz came to him, very strangely proud, and yet all tenderness.

"See, now, Raimbaut! because I have loved you as I have loved nothing else in life, I will not be unworthy of your love. Strike and have done."

Raimbaut de Vaquieras raised an already bloodied dagger. As emotion goes, he was bankrupt. He had no longer any dread of hell, because he thought that, a little later, nothing its shrewdest overseer could plan would have the power to vex him.

She, waiting, smiled. Makrisi, seated, stretched his legs, put fingertips together with the air of an attendant amateur. This was better than he had hoped. In such a posture they heard a bustle of armored men, and when all turned, saw how a sword protruded through the arras.

"Come out, Guillaume!" people were shouting. "Unkennel, dog! Out, out, and die!" To such a heralding Mahi de Vernoil came into the room with mincing steps such as the man affected in an hour of peril. He first saw what a grisly burden the chest sustained. "Now, by the Face!" he cried, "if he that cheated me of quieting this filth should prove to be of gentle birth I will demand of him a duel to the death!" The curtains were ripped from their hangings as he spoke, and behind him the candlelight was reflected by the armor of many followers.

Then de Vernoil perceived Raimbaut de Vaquieras, and the spruce little man bowed ceremoniously. All were still. Composedly, like a lieutenant before his captain, Mahi narrated how these hunted remnants of Lovain's army had, as a last cast, that night invaded the chateau, and had found, thanks to the festival, its men-at-arms in uniform and inefficient drunkenness. "My tres beau sire," Messire de Vernoil ended, "will you or nill you, Venaissin is yours this morning. My knaves have slain Philibert and his bewildered fellow-tipplers with less effort than is needed to drown as many kittens."

And his followers cried, as upon a signal: "Hail, Prince of Orange!"

It was so like the wonder-working of a dream--this sudden and heroic uproar--that old Raimbaut de Vaquieras stood reeling, near to intimacy with fear for the first time. He waited thus, with both hands pressed before his eyes. He waited thus for a long while, because he was not used to find chance dealing kindlily with him. Later he saw that Makrisi had vanished in the tumult, and that many people awaited his speaking.

The lord of Venaissin began: "You have done me a great service, Messire de Vemoil. As recompense, I give you what I may. I freely yield you all my right in Venaissin. Oh no, kingcraft is not for me. I daily see and hear of battles won, cities beleaguered, high towers overthrown, and ancient citadels and new walls leveled with the dust. I have conversed with many kings, the directors of these events, and they were not happy people. Yes, yes, I have witnessed divers happenings, for I am old. . . . I have found nothing which can serve me in place of honor."

He turned to Dona Biatritz. It was as if they were alone. "Belhs Cavaliers," he said, "I had sworn fealty to this Guillaume. He violated his obligations; but that did not free me of mine. An oath is an oath. I was, and am to-day, sworn to support his cause, and to profit in any fashion by its overthrow would be an abominable action. Nay, more, were any of his adherents alive it would be my manifest duty to join them against our preserver, Messire de Vernoil. This necessity is very happily spared me. I cannot, though, in honor hold any fief under the supplanter of my liege-lord. I must, therefore, relinquish Vaquieras and take eternal leave of Venaissin. I will not lose the right to call myself your servant!" he cried out--"and that which is noblest in the world must be served fittingly. And so, Belhs Cavaliers, let us touch palms and bid farewell, and never in this life speak face to face of trivial happenings which we two alone remember. For naked of lands and gear I came to you--a prince's daughter--very long ago, and as nakedly I now depart, so that I may retain the right to say, 'All my life long I served my love of her according to my abilities, wholeheartedly and with clean hands.'"

"Yes, yes! you must depart from Venaissin," said Dona Biatritz. A capable woman, she had no sympathy with his exquisite points of honor, and yet loved him all the more because of what seemed to her his surpassing folly. She smiled, somewhat as mothers do in humoring an unreasonable boy. "We will go to my nephew's court at Montferrat," she said. "He will willingly provide for his old aunt and her husband. And you may still make verses--at Montferrat, where we lived verses, once, Raimbaut."

Now they gazed full upon each other. Thus they stayed, transfigured, neither seeming old. Each had forgotten that unhappiness existed anywhere in the whole world. The armored, blood-stained men about them were of no more importance than were those wantons in the tapestry. Without, dawn throbbed in heaven. Without, innumerable birds were raising that glad, piercing, hurried morning-song which very anciently caused Adam's primal waking, to behold his mate.

BALTHAZAR'S DAUGHTER

A curious preference for the artificial should be mentioned as characteristic of ALESSANDRO DE MEDICI'S poetry. For his century was anything but artless; the great commonplaces that form the main stock of human thought were no longer in their first flush, and he addressed a people no longer childish. . . . Unquestionably his fancies were fantastic, anti-natural, bordering on hallucination, and they betray a desire for impossible novelty; but it is allowable to prefer them to the sickly simplicity of those so-called poems that embroider with old faded wools upon the canvas of worn-out truisms, trite, trivial and idiotically sentimental patterns."

Let me have dames and damsels richly clad
  To feed and tend my mirth,
Singing by day and night to make me glad;

Let me have fruitful gardens of great girth
  Fill'd with the strife of birds,
With water-springs, and beasts that house i' the earth.

Let me seem Solomon for lore of words,
Samson for strength, for beauty Absalom.

  Knights as my serfs be given;
And as I will, let music go and come;
Till, when I will, I will to enter Heaven.

ALESSANDRO DE MEDICI.--Madrigal, from D. G. Rossetti's version.

BALTHAZAR'S DAUGHTER

Graciosa was Balthazar's youngest child, a white, slim girl with violet eyes and strange pale hair which had the color and glitter of stardust. "Some day at court," her father often thought complacently, "she, too, will make a good match." He was a necessitous lord, a smiling, supple man who had already marketed two daughters to his advantage. But Graciosa's time was not yet mature in the year of grace 1533, for the girl was not quite sixteen. So Graciosa remained in Balthazar's big cheerless house and was tutored in all needful accomplishments. She was proficient in the making of preserves and unguents, could play the harpsichord and the virginals acceptably, could embroider an altarcloth to admiration, and, in spite of a trivial lameness in walking, could dance a coranto or a saraband against any woman between two seas.

Now to the north of Balthazar's home stood a tall forest, overhanging both the highway and the river whose windings the highway followed. Graciosa was very often to be encountered upon the outskirts of these woods. She loved the forest, whose tranquillity bred dreams, but was already a woman in so far that she found it more interesting to watch the highway. Sometimes it would be deserted save for small purple butterflies which fluttered about as if in continuous indecision, and rarely ascended more than a foot above the ground. But people passed at intervals--as now a page, who was a notably fine fellow, clothed in ash-colored gray, with slashed, puffed sleeves, and having a heron's feather in his cap; or a Franciscan with his gown tucked up so that you saw how the veins on his naked feet stood out like the carvings on a vase; or a farmer leading a calf; or a gentleman in a mantle of squirrel's fur riding beside a wonderful proud lady, whose tiny hat was embroidered with pearls. It was all very interesting to watch, it was like turning over the leaves of a book written in an unknown tongue and guessing what the pictures meant, because these people were intent upon their private avocations, in which you had no part, and you would never see them any more.

Then destiny took a hand in the affair and Guido came. He reined his gray horse at the sight of her sitting by the wayside and deferentially inquired how far it might be to the nearest inn. Graciosa told him. He thanked her and rode on. That was all, but the appraising glance of this sedate and handsome burgher obscurely troubled the girl afterward.

Next day he came again. He was a jewel-merchant, he told her, and he thought it within the stretch of possibility that my lord Balthazar's daughter might wish to purchase some of his wares. She viewed them with admiration, chaffered thriftily, and finally bought a topaz, dug from Mount Zabarca, Guido assured her, which rendered its wearer immune to terrors of any kind.

Very often afterward these two met on the outskirts of the forest as Guido rode between the coast and the hill-country about his vocation. Sometimes he laughingly offered her a bargain, on other days he paused to exhibit a notable gem which he had procured for this or that wealthy amateur. Count Eglamore, the young Duke's favorite yonder at court, bought most of them, it seemed. "The nobles complain against this upstart Eglamore very bitterly," said Guido, "but we merchants have no quarrel with him. He buys too lavishly."

"I trust I shall not see Count Eglamore when I go to court," said Graciosa, meditatively; "and, indeed, by that time, my father assures me, some honest gentleman will have contrived to cut the throat of this abominable Eglamore." Her father's people, it should be premised, had been at bitter feud with the favorite ever since he detected and punished the conspiracy of the Marquis of Cibo, their kinsman. Then Graciosa continued: "Nevertheless, I shall see many beautiful sights when I am taken to court. . . . And the Duke, too, you tell me, is an amateur of gems."

"Eh, madonna, I wish that you could see his jewels," cried Guido, growing fervent; and he lovingly catalogued a host of lapidary marvels.

"I hope that I shall see these wonderful jewels when I go to court," said Graciosa wistfully.

"Duke Alessandro," he returned, his dark eyes strangely mirthful, "is, as I take it, a catholic lover of beauty in all its forms. So he will show you his gems, very assuredly, and, worse still, he will make verses in your honor. For it is a preposterous feature of Duke Alessandro's character that he is always making songs."

"Oh, and such strange songs as they are, too, Guido. Who does not know them?"

"I am not the best possible judge of his verses' merit," Guido estimated, drily. "But I shall never understand how any singer at all came to be locked in such a prison. I fancy that at times the paradox puzzles even Duke Alessandro."

"And is he as handsome as people report?"

Then Guido laughed a little. "Tastes differ, of course. But I think your father will assure you, madonna, that no duke possessing such a zealous tax-collector as Count Eglamore was ever in his lifetime considered of repulsive person."

"And is he young?"

"Why, as to that, he is about of an age with me, and in consequence old enough to be far more sensible than either of us is ever likely to be," said Guido; and began to talk of other matters.

But presently Graciosa was questioning him again as to the court, whither she was to go next year and enslave a marquis, or, at worst, an opulent baron. Her thoughts turned toward the court's predominating figure. "Tell me of Eglamore, Guido."

"Madonna, some say that Eglamore was a brewer's son. Others--and your father's kinsmen in particular--insist that he was begot by a devil in person, just as Merlin was, and Plato the philosopher, and puissant Alexander. Nobody knows anything about his origin." Guido was sitting upon the ground, his open pack between his knees. Between the thumb and forefinger of each hand he held caressingly a string of pearls which he inspected as he talked. "Nobody," he idly said, "nobody is very eager to discuss Count Eglamore's origin now that Eglamore has become indispensable to Duke Alessandro. Yes, it is thanks to Eglamore that the Duke has ample leisure and needful privacy for the pursuit of recreations which are reputed to be curious."

"I do not understand you, Guido." Graciosa was all wonder.

"It is perhaps as well," the merchant said, a trifle sadly. Then Guido shrugged. "To be brief, madonna, business annoys the Duke. He finds in this Eglamore an industrious person who affixes seals, draughts proclamations, makes treaties, musters armies, devises pageants, and collects revenues, upon the whole, quite as efficiently as Alessandro would be capable of doing these things. So Alessandro makes verses and amuses himself as his inclinations prompt, and Alessandro's people are none the worse off on account of it."

"Heigho, I foresee that I shall never fall in love with the Duke," Graciosa declared. "It is unbefitting and it is a little cowardly for a prince to shirk the duties of his station. Now, if I were Duke I would grant my father a pension, and have Eglamore hanged, and purchase a new gown of silvery green, in which I would be ravishingly beautiful, and afterward-- Why, what would you do if you were Duke, Messer Guido?"

"What would I do if I were Duke?" he echoed. "What would I do if I were a great lord instead of a tradesman? I think you know the answer, madonna."

"Oh, you would make me your duchess, of course. That is quite understood," said Graciosa, with the lightest of laughs. "But I was speaking seriously, Guido."

Guido at that considered her intently for a half-minute. His countenance was of portentous gravity, but in his eyes she seemed to detect a lurking impishness.

"And it is not a serious matter that a peddler of crystals should have dared to love a nobleman's daughter? You are perfectly right. That I worship you is an affair which does not concern any person save myself in any way whatsoever, although I think that knowledge of the fact would put your father to the trouble of sharpening his dagger. . . . Indeed, I am not certain that I worship you, for in order to adore wholeheartedly, the idolater must believe his idol to be perfect. Now, your nails are of an ugly shape, like that of little fans; your mouth is too large; and I have long ago perceived that you are a trifle lame in spite of your constant care to conceal the fact. I do not admire these faults, for faults they are undoubtedly. Then, too, I know you are vain and self-seeking, and look forward contentedly to the time when your father will transfer his ownership of such physical attractions as heaven gave you to that nobleman who offers the highest price for them. It is true you have no choice in the matter, but you will participate in a monstrous bargain, and I would prefer to have you exhibit distaste for it." And with that he returned composedly to inspection of his pearls.

"And to what end, Guido?" It was the first time Graciosa had completely waived the reticence of a superior caste. You saw that the child's parted lips were tremulous, and you divined her childish fits of dreading that glittering, inevitable court-life shared with an unimaginable husband.

But Guido only grumbled whimsically. "I am afraid that men do not always love according to the strict laws of logic. I desire your happiness above all things;

yet to see you so abysmally untroubled by anything that troubles me is another matter."

"But I am not untroubled, Guido----" she began swiftly. Graciosa broke off in speech, shrugged, flashed a smile at him. "For I cannot fathom you, Ser Guido, and that troubles me. Yes, I am very fond of you, and yet I do not trust you. You tell me you love me greatly. It pleases me to have you say this. You perceive I am very candid this morning, Messer Guido. Yes, it pleases me, and I know that for the sake of seeing me you daily endanger your life, for if my father heard of our meetings he would have you killed. You would not incur such hare-brained risks unless you cared very greatly; and yet, somehow, I do not believe it is altogether for me you care."

Then Guido was in train to protest an all-mastering and entirely candid devotion, but he was interrupted.

"Most women have these awkward intuitions," spoke a melodious voice, and turning, Graciosa met the eyes of the intruder. This magnificent young man had a proud and bloodless face which contrasted sharply with his painted lips and cheeks. In the contour of his protruding mouth showed plainly his negroid ancestry. His scanty beard, as well as his frizzled hair, was the color of dead grass. He was sumptuously clothed in white satin worked with silver, and around his cap was a gold chain hung with diamonds. Now he handed his fringed riding-gloves to Guido to hold.

"Yes, madonna, I suspect that Eglamore here cares greatly for the fact that you are Lord Balthazar's daughter, and cousin to the late Marquis of Cibo. For Cibo has many kinsmen at court who still resent the circumstance that the matching of his wits against Eglamore's earned for Cibo a deplorably public demise. So they conspire against Eglamore with vexatious industry, as an upstart, as a nobody thrust over people of proven descent, and Eglamore goes about in hourly apprehension of a knife-thrust. If he could make a match with you, though, your father--thrifty man!--would be easily appeased. Your cousins, those proud, grumbling Castel-Franchi, Strossi and Valori, would not prove over-obdurate toward a kinsman who, whatever his past indiscretions, has so many pensions and offices at his disposal. Yes, honor would permit a truce, and Eglamore could bind them to his interests within ten days, and be rid of the necessity of sleeping in chain armor. . . . Have I not unraveled the scheme correctly, Eglamore?"

"Your highness was never lacking in penetration," replied the other in a dull voice. He stood motionless, holding the gloves, his shoulders a little bowed as if under some physical load. His eyes were fixed upon the ground. He divined the change in Graciosa's face and did not care to see it.

"And so you are Count Eglamore," said Graciosa in a sort of whisper. "That is very strange. I had thought you were my friend, Guido. But I forget. I must not call you Guido any longer." She gave a little shiver here. He stayed motionless and did not look at her. "I have often wondered what manner of man you were. So it was you--whose hand I touched just now--you who poisoned Duke Cosmo, you who had the good cardinal assassinated, you who betrayed the brave lord of Faenza! Oh, yes, they openly accuse you of every imaginable crime--this patient Eglamore, this reptile who has crept into his power through filthy passages. It is very strange you should be capable of so much wickedness, for to me you seem only a sullen lackey."

He winced and raised his eyes at this. His face remained expressionless. He knew these accusations at least to be demonstrable lies, for as it happened he had never found his advancement to hinge upon the commission of the crimes named. But even so, the past was a cemetery he did not care to have revivified.

"And it was you who detected the Marquis of Cibo's conspiracy. Tebaldeo was my cousin, Count Eglamore, and I loved him. We were reared together. We used to play here in these woods, and I remember how Tebaldeo once fetched me a wren's nest from that maple yonder. I stood just here. I was weeping because I was afraid he would fall. If he had fallen and been killed, it would have been the luckier for him," Graciosa sighed. "They say that he conspired. I do not know. I only know that by your orders, Count Eglamore, my playmate Tebaldeo was fastened upon a Saint Andrew's cross and his arms and legs were each broken in two places with an iron bar. Then your servants took Tebaldeo, still living, and laid him upon a carriage-wheel which was hung upon a pivot. The upper edge of this wheel was cut with very fine teeth like those of a saw, so that his agony might be complete. Tebaldeo's poor mangled legs were folded beneath his body so that his heels touched the back of his head, they tell me. In such a posture he died very slowly while the wheel turned very slowly there in the sunlit market-place, and flies buzzed greedily about him, and the shopkeepers took holiday in order to watch Tebaldeo die--the same Tebaldeo who once fetched me a wren's nest from yonder maple."

Eglamore spoke now. "I gave orders for the Marquis of Cibo's execution. I did not devise the manner of his death. The punishment for Cibo's crime was long ago fixed by our laws. Cibo plotted to kill the Duke. Cibo confessed as much."

But the girl waved this aside. "And then you plan this masquerade. You plan to make me care for you so greatly that even when I know you to be Count Eglamore I must still care for you. You plan to marry me, so as to placate Tebaldeo's kinsmen, so as to bind them to your interests. It was a fine bold stroke of policy, I know, to use me as a stepping-stone to safety--but was it fair to me?" Her voice rose now a little. She seemed to plead with him. "Look you, Count Eglamore, I was a child only yesterday. I have never loved any man. But you have loved many women, I know, and long experience has taught you many ways of moving a woman's heart. Oh, was it fair, was it worth while, to match your skill against my ignorance? Think how unhappy I would be if even now I loved you, and how I would loathe myself. . . . But I am getting angry over nothing. Nothing has happened except that I have dreamed in idle moments of a brave and comely lover who held his head so high that all other women envied me, and now I have awakened."

Meanwhile, it was with tears in his eyes that the young man in white had listened to her quiet talk, for you could nowhere have found a nature more readily sensitive than his to all the beauty and wonder which life, as if it were haphazardly, produces every day. He pitied this betrayed child quite ineffably, because in her sorrow she was so pretty.

So he spoke consolingly. "Fie, Donna Graciosa, you must not be too harsh with Eglamore. It is his nature to scheme, and he weaves his plots as inevitably as the spider does her web. Believe me, it is wiser to forget the rascal--as I do--until there is need of him; and I think you will have no more need to consider Eglamore's trickeries, for you are very beautiful, Graciosa."

He had drawn closer to the girl, and he brought a cloying odor of frangipani, bergamot and vervain. His nostrils quivered, his face had taken on an odd pinched look, for all that he smiled as over some occult jest. Graciosa was a little frightened by his bearing, which was both furtive and predatory.

"Oh, do not be offended, for I have some rights to say what I desire in these parts. For, ***Dei gratia***, I am the overlord of these parts, Graciosa--a neglected prince who wondered over the frequent absences of his chief counselor and secretly set spies upon him. Eglamore here will attest as much. Or if you cannot believe poor Eglamore any longer, I shall have other witnesses within the half-hour. Oh, yes, they are to meet me here at noon--some twenty crop-haired stalwart cut-throats. They will come riding upon beautiful broad-chested horses covered with red velvet trappings that are hung with little silver bells which jingle delightfully. They will come very soon, and then we will ride back to court."

Duke Alessandro touched his big painted mouth with his forefinger as if in fantastic mimicry of a man imparting a confidence.

"I think that I shall take you with me, Graciosa, for you are very beautiful. You are as slim as a lily and more white, and your eyes are two purple mirrors in each of which I see a tiny image of Duke Alessandro. The woman I loved yesterday was a big splendid wench with cheeks like apples. It is not desirable that women should be so large. All women should be little creatures that fear you. They should have thin, plaintive voices, and in shrinking from you be as slight to the touch as a cob-web. It is not possible to love a woman ardently unless you comprehend how easy it would be to murder her."

"God, God!" said Count Eglamore, very softly, for he was familiar with the look which had now come into Duke Alessandro's face. Indeed, all persons about court were quick to notice this odd pinched look, like that of a traveler nipped at by frosts, and people at court became obsequious within the instant in dealing with the fortunate woman who had aroused this look, Count Eglamore remembered.

And the girl did not speak at all, but stood motionless, staring in bewildered, pitiable, childlike fashion, and the color had ebbed from her countenance.

Alessandro was frankly pleased. "You fear me, do you not, Graciosa? See, now, when I touch your hand it is soft and cold as a serpent's skin, and you shudder. I am very tired of women who love me, of all women with bold, hungry eyes. To you my touch will always be a martyrdom, you will always loathe me, and therefore I shall not weary of you for a long while. Come, Graciosa. Your father shall have all the wealth and state that even his greedy imaginings can devise, so long as you can contrive to loathe me. We will find you a suitable husband. You shall have flattery and titles, gold and fine glass, soft stuffs and superb palaces such as are your beauty's due henceforward."

He glanced at the peddler's pack, and shrugged. "So Eglamore has been woo-ing you with jewels! You must see mine, dear Graciosa. It is not merely an affair of possessing, as some emperors do, all the four kinds of sapphires, the twelve kinds of emeralds, the three kinds of rubies, and many extraordinary pearls, diamonds, cy-mophanes, beryls, green peridots, tyanos, sandrastra, and fiery cinnamon-stones"--he enumerated them with the tender voice of their lover--"for the value of these may at least be estimated. Oh, no, I have in my possession gems which have not their fellows in any other collection, gems which have not even a name and the value of which is incalculable--strange jewels that were shot from inaccessible mountain peaks by means of slings, jewels engendered by the thunder, jewels taken from the heart of the Arabian deer, jewels cut from the brain of a toad and the eyes of serpents, and even jewels that are authentically known to have fallen from the moon. We will select the rarest, and have a pair of slippers encrusted with them, in which you shall dance for me."

"Highness," cried Eglamore, with anger and terror at odds in his breast, "High-ness, I love this girl!"

"Ah, then you cannot ever be her husband," Duke Alessandro returned. "You would have suited otherwise. No, no, we must seek out some other person of dis-cretion. It will all be very amusing, for I think that she is now quite innocent, as pure as the high angels are. See, Eglamore, she cannot speak, she stays still as a lark that has been taken in a snare. It will be very marvelous to make her as I am. . . ." He meditated, as, obscurely aware of opposition, his shoulders twitched fretfully, and momentarily his eyes lightened like the glare of a cannon through its smoke. "You made a beast of me, some long-faced people say. Beware lest the beast turn and rend you."

Count Eglamore plucked aimlessly at his chin. Then he laughed as a dog yelps. He dropped the gloves which he had held till this, deliberately, as if the act were a rite. His shoulders straightened and purpose seemed to flow into the man. "No," he said quietly, "I will not have it. It was not altogether I who made a brain-sick beast of you, my prince; but even so, I have never been too nice to profit by your vices. I have taken my thrifty toll of abomination, I have stood by contentedly, not urging you on, yet never trying to stay you, as you waded deeper and ever deeper into the filth of your debaucheries, because meanwhile you left me so much power. Yes, in some part it is my own handiwork which is my ruin. I accept it. Nevertheless, you shall not harm this child."

"I venture to remind you, Eglamore, that I am still the master of this duchy." Alessandro was languidly amused, and had begun to regard his adversary with real curiosity.

"Oh, yes, but that is nothing to me. At court you are the master. At court I have seen mothers raise the veil from their daughters' faces, with smiles that were more loathsome than the grimaces of a fiend, because you happened to be passing. But here in these woods, your highness, I see only the woman I love and the man who has insulted her."

"This is very admirable fooling," the Duke considered. "So all the world is changed and Pandarus is transformed into Hector? These are sonorous words, Eglamore, but with what deeds do you propose to back them?"

"By killing you, your highness."

"So!" said the Duke. "The farce ascends in interest." He drew with a flourish, with actual animation, for sottish, debauched and power-crazed as this man was, he came of a race to whom danger was a cordial. "Very luckily a sword forms part of your disguise, so let us amuse ourselves. It is always diverting to kill, and if by any chance you kill me I shall at least be rid of the intolerable knowledge that to-morrow will be just like to-day." The Duke descended blithely into the level road and placed himself on guard.

Then both men silently went about the business in hand. Both were oddly calm, almost as if preoccupied by some more important matter to be settled later. The two swords clashed, gleamed rigidly for an instant, and then their rapid interplay, so far as vision went, melted into a flickering snarl of silver, for the sun was high and each man's shadow was huddled under him. Then Eglamore thrust savagely and in the act trod the edge of a puddle, and fell ignominiously prostrate. His sword was wrenched ten feet from him, for the Duke had parried skilfully. Eglamore lay thus at Alessandro's mercy.

"Well, well!" the Duke cried petulantly, "and am I to be kept waiting forever? You were a thought quicker in obeying my caprices yesterday. Get up, you muddy lout, and let us kill each other with some pretension of adroitness."

Eglamore rose, and, sobbing, caught up his sword and rushed toward the Duke in an agony of shame and rage. His attack now was that of a frenzied animal, quite careless of defense and desirous only of murder. Twice the Duke wounded him, but it was Alessandro who drew backward, composedly hindering the brutal onslaught he was powerless to check. Then Eglamore ran him through the chest and gave vent to a strangled, growling cry as Alessandro fell. Eglamore wrenched his sword free and grasped it by the blade so that he might stab the Duke again and again. He meant to hack the abominable flesh, to slash and mutilate that haughty mask of infamy, but Graciosa clutched his weapon by the hilt.

The girl panted, and her breath came thick. "He gave you your life."

Eglamore looked up. She leaned now upon his shoulder, her face brushing his as he knelt over the unconscious Duke; and Eglamore found that at her dear touch all passion had gone out of him.

"Madonna," he said equably, "the Duke is not yet dead. It is impossible to let him live. You may think he voiced only a caprice just now. I think so too, but I know the man, and I know that all this madman's whims are ruthless and irresistible. Living, Duke Alessandro's appetites are merely whetted by opposition, so much so that he finds no pleasures sufficiently piquant unless they have God's interdiction as a sauce. Living, he will make of you his plaything, and a little later his broken, soiled and castby plaything. It is therefore necessary that I kill Duke Alessandro."

She parted from him, and he too rose to his feet.

"And afterward," she said quietly, "and afterward you must die just as Tebaldeo died."

"That is the law, madonna. But whether Alessandro enters hell to-day or later, I am a lost man."

"Oh, that is very true," she said. "A moment since you were Count Eglamore, whom every person feared. Now there is not a beggar in the kingdom who would change lots with you, for you are a friendless and hunted man in peril of dreadful death. But even so, you are not penniless, Count Eglamore, for these jewels here which formed part of your masquerade are of great value, and there is a world outside. The frontier is not two miles distant. You have only to escape into the hill-country beyond the forest, and you need not kill Duke Alessandro after all. I would have you go hence with hands as clean as possible."

"Perhaps I might escape." He found it quaint to note how calm she was and how tranquilly his own thoughts ran. "But first the Duke must die, because I dare not leave you to his mercy."

"How does that matter?" she returned. "You know very well that my father intends to market me as best suits his interests. Here I am so much merchandise. The Duke is as free as any other man to cry a bargain." He would have spoken in protest, but Graciosa interrupted wearily: "Oh, yes, it is to this end only that we daughters of Duke Alessandro's vassals are nurtured, just as you told me--eh, how long ago!-- that such physical attractions as heaven accords us may be marketed. And I do not see how a wedding can in any way ennoble the transaction by causing it to profane a holy sacrament. Ah, no, Balthazar's daughter was near attaining all that she had been taught to desire, for a purchaser came and he bid lavishly. You know very well that my father would have been delighted. But you must need upset the bargain. 'No, I will not have it!' Count Eglamore must cry. It cost you very highly to speak those words. I think it would have puzzled my father to hear those words at which so many fertile lands, stout castles, well-timbered woodlands, herds of cattle, gilded coaches, liveries and curious tapestries, fine clothing and spiced foods, all vanished like a puff of smoke. Ah, yes, my father would have thought you mad."

"I had no choice," he said, and waved a little gesture of impotence. He spoke as with difficulty, almost wearily. "I love you. It is a theme on which I do not embroider. So long as I had thought to use you as an instrument I could woo fluently enough. To-day I saw that you were frightened and helpless--oh, quite helpless. And something changed in me. I knew for the first time that I loved you and that I was not clean as you are clean. What it was of passion and horror, of despair and adoration and yearning, which struggled in my being then I cannot tell you. It spurred me to such action as I took,--but it has robbed me of sugared eloquence, it has left me chary of speech. It is necessary that I climb very high because of my love for you, and upon the heights there is silence."

And Graciosa meditated. "Here I am so much merchandise. Heigho, since I cannot help it, since bought and sold I must be, one day or another, at least I will go at a noble price. Yet I do not think I am quite worth the value of these castles and lands and other things which you gave up because of me, so that it will be necessary to make up the difference, dear, by loving you very much."

And at that he touched her chin, gently and masterfully, for Graciosa would have averted her face, and it seemed to Eglamore that he could never have his fill of gazing on the radiant, shamed tenderness of Graciosa's face. "Oh, my girl!" he whispered. "Oh, my wonderful, worshiped, merry girl, whom God has fashioned with such loving care! you who had only scorn to give me when I was a kingdom's master! and would you go with me now that I am friendless and homeless?"

"But I shall always have a friend," she answered--"a friend who showed me what Balthazar's daughter was and what love is. And I am vain enough to believe I shall not ever be very far from home so long as I am near to my friend's heart."

A mortal man could not but take her in his arms.

"Farewell, Duke Alessandro!" then said Eglamore; "farewell, poor clay so plastic the least touch remodels you! I had a part in shaping you so bestial; our age, too, had a part--our bright and cruel day, wherein you were set too high. Yet for me it would perhaps have proved as easy to have made a learned recluse of you, Alessandro, or a bloodless saint, if to do that had been as patently profitable. For you and all your kind are so much putty in the hands of circumspect fellows such as I. But I stood by and let our poisoned age conform that putty into the shape of a crazed beast, because it took that form as readily as any other, and in taking it, best served my selfish ends. Now I must pay for that sorry shaping, just as, I think, you too must pay some day. And so, I cry farewell with loathing, but with compassion also!"

Then these two turned toward the hills, leaving Duke Alessandro where he lay in the road, a very lamentable figure in much bloodied finery. They turned toward the hills, and entered a forest whose ordering was time's contemporary, and where there was no grandeur save that of the trees.

But upon the summit of the nearest hill they paused and looked over a restless welter of foliage that glittered in the sun, far down into the highway. It bustled like an unroofed ant-hill, for the road was alive with men who seemed from this distance very small. Duke Alessandro's attendants had found him and were clustered in a hubbub about their reviving master. Dwarfish Lorenzino de Medici was the most solicitous among them.

Beyond was the broad river, seen as a ribbon of silver now, and on its remoter bank the leaded roofs of a strong fortress glistened like a child's new toy. Tilled fields showed here and there, no larger in appearance than so many outspread handkerchiefs. Far down in the east a small black smudge upon the pearl-colored and vaporous horizon was all they could discern of a walled city filled with factories for the working of hemp and furs and alum and silk and bitumen.

"It is a very rich and lovely land," said Eglamore--"this kingdom which a half-hour since lay in the hollow of my hand." He viewed it for a while, and not without pensiveness. Then he took Graciosa's hand and looked into her face, and he laughed joyously.

JUDITH'S CREED

It does not appear that the age thought his works worthy of posterity, nor that this great poet himself levied any ideal tribute on future times, or had any further prospect than of present popularity and present profit. So careless was he, indeed, of fame, that, when he retired to ease and plenty, while he was yet little declined into the vale of years, and before he could be disgusted with fatigue or disabled by infirmity, he desired only that in this rural quiet he who had so long mazed his imagination by following phantoms might at last be cured of his delirious ecstasies, and as a hermit might estimate the transactions of the world."

Now my charms are all o'erthrown,
And what strength I have's my own,
Which is most faint.

       Now I want
Spirits to enforce, art to enchant;
And my ending is despair,
Unless I be relieved by prayer,
Which pierces so, that it assaults
Mercy itself, and frees all faults.

As you from crimes would pardon'd be,
Let your indulgence set me free.

WILLIAM SHAKESPEARE.--Epilogue to The Tempest.

He was hoping, while his fingers drummed in unison with the beat of his verse, that this last play at least would rouse enthusiasm in the pit. The welcome given its immediate predecessors had undeniably been tepid. A memorandum at his elbow of the receipts at the Globe for the last quarter showed this with disastrous bluntness; and, after all, in 1609 a shareholder in a theater, when writing dramas for production there, was ordinarily subject to more claims than those of his ideals.

He sat in a neglected garden whose growth was in reversion to primal habits. The season was September, the sky a uniform and temperate blue. A peachtree, laden past its strength with fruitage, made about him with its boughs a sort of tent. The grass around his writing-table was largely hidden by long, crinkled peach leaves--some brown and others gray as yet--and was dotted with a host of brightly-colored peaches. Fidgeting bees and flies were excavating the decayed spots in this wasting fruit, from which emanated a vinous odor. The bees hummed drowsily, their industry facilitating idleness in others. It was curious--he meditated, his thoughts straying from "an uninhabited island"--how these insects alternated in color between brown velvet and silver, as they blundered about a flickering tessellation of amber and dark green . . . in search of rottenness. . . .

He frowned. Here was an arid forenoon as imagination went. A seasoned plagiarist by this, he opened a book which lay upon the table among several others and duly found the chapter entitled *Of the Cannibals*.

"So, so!" he said aloud. "'It is a nation,' would I answer Plato, 'that has no kind of traffic, no knowledge of letters----'" And with that he sat about reshaping Montaigne's conceptions of Utopia into verse. He wrote--while his left hand held the book flat--as orderly as any county-clerk might do in the recordance of a deed of sale.

Midcourse in larceny, he looked up from writing. He saw a tall, dark lady who was regarding him half-sorrowfully and half as in the grasp of some occult amusement. He said nothing. He released the telltale book. His eyebrows lifted, banteringly. He rose.

He found it characteristic of her that she went silently to the table and compared the printed page with what he had just written. "So nowadays you have turned pickpocket? My poet, you have altered."

He said: "Why, yes. When you broke off our friendship, I paid you the expensive compliment of falling very ill. They thought that I would die. They tell me even to-day I did not die. I almost question it." He shrugged. "And to-day I must continue to write plays, because I never learned any other trade. And so, at need, I pilfer." The topic did not seem much to concern him.

"Eh, and such plays!" the woman cried. "My poet, there was a time when you created men and women as glibly as Heaven does. Now you make sugar-candy dolls."

"The last comedies were not all I could have wished," he assented. "In fact, I got only some L30 clear profit."

"There speaks the little tradesman I most hated of all persons living!" the woman sighed. Now, as in impatience, she thrust back her traveling-hood and stood bare-headed.

Then she stayed silent,--tall, extraordinarily pallid, and with dark, steady eyes. Their gaze by ordinary troubled you, as seeming to hint some knowledge to your belittlement. The playmaker remembered that. Now he, a reputable householder, was wondering what would be the upshot of this intrusion. His visitor, as he was perfectly aware, had little patience with such moments of life as could not be made dramatic. . . . He was recollecting many trifles, now his mind ran upon old times. . . . No, no, reflection assured him, to call her beautiful would be, and must always have been, an exaggeration; but to deny the exotic and somewhat sinister charm of her, even to-day, would be an absurdity.

She said, abruptly: "I do not think I ever loved you as women love men. You were too anxious to associate with fine folk, too eager to secure a patron--yes, and to get your profit of him--and you were always ill-at-ease among us. Our youth is so long past, and we two are so altered that we, I think, may speak of its happenings now without any bitterness. I hated those sordid, petty traits. I raged at your incessant pretensions to gentility because I knew you to be so much more than a gentleman. Oh, it infuriated me--how long ago it was!--to see you cringing to the Court blockheads, and running their errands, and smirkingly pocketing their money, and wheedling them into helping the new play to success. You complained I treated you like a lackey; it was not unnatural when of your own freewill you played the lackey so assiduously."

He laughed. He had anatomized himself too frequently and with too much dispassion to overlook whatever tang of snobbishness might be in him; and, moreover, the charge thus tendered became in reality the speaker's apology, and hurt nobody's self-esteem.

"Faith, I do not say you are altogether in the wrong," he assented. "They could be very useful to me--Pembroke, and Southampton, and those others--and so I endeavored to render my intimacy acceptable. It was my business as a poet to make my play as near perfect as I could; and this attended to, common-sense demanded of the theater-manager that he derive as much money as was possible from its representation. What would you have? The man of letters, like the carpenter or the blacksmith, must live by the vending of his productions, not by the eating of them." The woman waved this aside.

She paced the grass in meditation, the peach leaves brushing her proud head--caressingly, it seemed to him. Later she came nearer in a brand-new mood. She smiled now, and her voice was musical and thrilled with wonder. "But what a poet Heaven had locked inside this little parasite! It used to puzzle me." She laughed, and ever so lightly. "Eh, and did you never understand why by preference I talked with you at evening from my balcony? It was because I could forget you then entirely. There was only a voice in the dark. There was a sorcerer at whose bidding words trooped like a conclave of emperors, and now sang like a bevy of linnets. And wit and fancy and high aspirations and my love--because I knew then that your love for me was splendid and divine--these also were my sorcerer's potent allies. I understood then how glad and awed were those fabulous Greekish queens when a god wooed them. Yes, then I understood. How long ago it seems!"

"Yes, yes," he sighed. "In that full-blooded season was Guenevere a lass, I think, and Charlemagne was not yet in breeches."

"And when there was a new play enacted I was glad. For it was our play that you and I had polished the last line of yesterday, and all these people wept and laughed because of what we had done. And I was proud----" The lady shrugged impatiently. "Proud, did I say? and glad? That attests how woefully I fall short of you, my poet. You would have found some magic phrase to make that ancient glory articulate, I know. Yet,--did I ever love you? I do not know that. I only know I sometimes fear you robbed me of the power of loving any other man."

He raised one hand in deprecation. "I must remind you," he cried, whimsically, "that a burnt child dreads even to talk of fire."

Her response was a friendly nod. She came yet nearer. "What," she demanded, and her smile was elfish, "what if I had lied to you? What if I were hideously tired of my husband, that bluff, stolid captain? What if I wanted you to plead with me as in the old time?"

He said: "Until now you were only a woman. Oh, and now, my dear, you are again that resistless gipsy who so merrily beguiled me to the very heart of loss. You are Love. You are Youth. You are Comprehension. You are all that I have had, and lost, and vainly hunger for. Here in this abominable village, there is no one who understands--not even those who are more dear to me than you are. I know. I only spoil good paper which might otherwise be profitably used to wrap herrings in, they think. They give me ink and a pen just as they would give toys to a child who squalled for them too obstinately. And Poesy is a thrifty oracle with no words to waste upon the deaf, however loudly her interpreter cry out to her. Oh, I have hungered for you, my proud, dark lady!" the playmaker said.

Afterward they stood quite silent. She was not unmoved by his outcry; and for this very reason was obscurely vexed by the reflection that it would be the essay of a braver man to remedy, rather than to lament, his circumstances. And then the moment's rapture failed him.

"I am a sorry fool," he said; and lightly he ran on: "You are a skilful witch. Yet you have raised the ghost of an old madness to no purpose. You seek a master-poet? You will find none here. Perhaps I was one once. But most of us are poets of one sort or another when we love. Do you not understand? To-day I do not love you any more than I do Hecuba. Is it not strange that I should tell you this and not be moved at all? Is it not laughable that we should stand here at the last, two feet apart as things physical go, and be as profoundly severed as if an ocean tumbled between us?"

He fell to walking to and fro, his hands behind his back. She waited, used as she was to his unstable temperament, a trifle puzzled. Presently he spoke:

"There was a time when a master-poet was needed. He was found--nay,--rather made. Fate hastily caught up a man not very different from the run of men--one with a taste for stringing phrases and with a comedy or so to his discredit. Fate merely bid him love a headstrong child newly released from the nursery."

"We know her well enough," she said. "The girl was faithless, and tyrannous, and proud, and coquettish, and unworthy, and false, and inconstant. She was black as hell and dark as night in both her person and her living. You were not niggardly of vituperation."

And he grimaced. "Faith," he replied, "but sonnets are a more natural form of expression than affidavits, and they are made effective by compliance with different rules. I find no flagrant fault with you to-day. You were a child of seventeen, the darling of a noble house, and an actor--yes, and not even a pre-eminent actor--a gross, poor posturing vagabond, just twice your age, presumed to love you. What child would not amuse herself with such engaging toys? Vivacity and prettiness and cruelty are the ordinary attributes of kittenhood. So you amused yourself. And I submitted with clear eyes, because I could not help it. Yes, I who am by nature not disposed to underestimate my personal importance--I submitted, because your mockery was more desirable than the adoration of any other woman. And all this helped to make a master-poet of me. Eh, why not, when such monstrous passions spoke through me--as if some implacable god elected to play godlike music on a mountebank's lute? And I made admirable plays. Why not, when there was no tragedy more poignant than mine?--and where in any comedy was any figure one-half so ludicrous as mine? Ah, yes, Fate gained her ends, as always."

He was a paunchy, inconsiderable little man. By ordinary his elongated features and high, bald forehead loaned him an aspect of serene and axiom-based wisdom, much as we see him in his portraits; but now his countenance was flushed and mobile. Odd passions played about it, as when on a sullen night in August summer lightnings flicker and merge.

His voice had found another cadence. "But Fate was not entirely ruthless. Fate bade the child become a woman, and so grow tired of all her childhood's playthings. This was after a long while, as we estimate happenings. . . . I suffered then. Yes, I went down to the doors of death, as people say, in my long illness. But that crude, corporal fever had a providential thievishness; and not content with stripping me of health and strength,--not satisfied with pilfering inventiveness and any strong hunger to create--why, that insatiable fever even robbed me of my insanity. I lived. I was only a broken instrument flung by because the god had wearied of playing. I would give forth no more heart-wringing music, for the musician had departed. And I still lived--I, the stout little tradesman whom you loathed. Yes, that tradesman scrambled through these evils, somehow, and came out still able to word adequately all such imaginings as could be devised by his natural abilities. But he transmitted no more heart-wringing music."

She said, "You lie!"

He said, "I thank Heaven daily that I do not." He spoke the truth. She knew it, and her heart was all rebellion.

Indefatigable birds sang through the following hush. A wholesome and temperate breeze caressed these silent people. Bees that would die to-morrow hummed about them tirelessly.

Then the poet said: "I loved you; and you did not love me. It is the most commonplace of tragedies, the heart of every man alive has been wounded in this identical fashion. A master-poet is only that wounded man--among so many other bleeding folk--who perversely augments his agony, and utilizes his wound as an inkwell. Presently time scars over the cut for him, as time does for all the others. He does not suffer any longer. No, and such relief is a clear gain; but none the less, he must henceforward write with ordinary ink such as the lawyers use."

"I should have been the man," the woman cried. "Had I been sure of fame, could I have known those raptures when you used to gabble immortal phrases like a stammering infant, I would have paid the price without all this whimpering."

"Faith, and I think you would have," he assented. "There is the difference. At bottom I am a creature of the most moderate aspirations, as you always complained; and for my part, Fate must in reason demand her applause of posterity rather than of me. For I regret the unlived life that I was meant for--the comfortable level life of little happenings which all my schoolfellows have passed through in a stolid drove. I was equipped to live that life with relish, and that life only; and it was denied me. It was demolished in order that a book or two be made out of its wreckage."

She said, with half-shut eyes: "There is a woman at the root of all this." And how he laughed!

"Did I not say you were a witch? Why, most assuredly there is."

He motioned with his left hand. Some hundred yards away a young man, who was carrying two logs toward New Place, had paused to rest. A girl was with him. Now laughingly she was pretending to assist the porter in lifting his burden. It was a quaintly pretty vignette, as framed by the peach leaves, because those two young people were so merry and so candidly in love. A symbolist might have wrung pathos out of the girl's desire to aid, as set against her fond inadequacy; and the attendant playwright made note of it.

"Well, well!" he said: "Young Quiney is a so-so choice, since women must necessarily condescend to intermarrying with men. But he is far from worthy of her. Tell me, now, was there ever a rarer piece of beauty?"

"The wench is not ill-favored," was the dark lady's unenthusiastic answer. "So!--but who is she?"

He replied: "She is my daughter. Yonder you see my latter muse for whose dear sake I spin romances. I do not mean that she takes any lively interest in them. That is not to be expected, since she cannot read or write. Ask her about the poet we were discussing, and I very much fear Judith will bluntly inform you she cannot tell a B from a bull's foot. But one must have a muse of some sort or another; and so I write about the world now as Judith sees it. My Judith finds this world an eminently pleasant place. It is full of laughter and kindliness--for could Herod be unkind to her?--and it is largely populated by ardent young fellows who are intended chiefly to be twisted about your fingers; and it is illuminated by sunlight whose real purpose is to show how pretty your hair is. And if affairs go badly for a while, and you have done nothing very wrong--why, of course, Heaven will soon straighten matters satisfactorily. For nothing that happens to us can possibly be anything except a benefit, because God orders all happenings, and God loves us. There you have Judith's creed; and upon my word, I believe there is a great deal to be said for it."

"And this is you," she cried--"you who wrote of Troilus and Timon!"

"I lived all that," he replied--"I lived it, and so for a long while I believed in the existence of wickedness. To-day I have lost many illusions, madam, and that ranks among them. I never knew a wicked person. I question if anybody ever did. Undoubtedly short-sighted people exist who have floundered into ill-doing; but it proves always to have been on account of either cowardice or folly, and never because of malevolence; and, in consequence, their sorry pickle should demand commiseration far more loudly than our blame. In short, I find humanity to be both a weaker and a better-meaning race than I had suspected. And so, I make what you call 'sugar-candy dolls,' because I very potently believe that all of us are sweet at heart. Oh no! men lack an innate aptitude for sinning; and at worst, we frenziedly attempt our misdemeanors just as a sheep retaliates on its pursuers. This much, at least, has Judith taught me."

The woman murmured: "Eh, you are luckier than I. I had a son. He was borne of my anguish, he was fed and tended by me, and he was dependent on me in all things." She said, with a half-sob, "My poet, he was so little and so helpless! Now he is dead."

"My dear, my dear!" he cried, and he took both her hands. "I also had a son. He would have been a man by this."

They stood thus for a while. And then he smiled.

"I ask your pardon. I had forgotten that you hate to touch my hands. I know--they are too moist and flabby. I always knew that you thought that. Well! Hamnet died. I grieved. That is a trivial thing to say. But you also have seen your own flesh lying in a coffin so small that even my soft hands could lift it. So you will comprehend. To-day I find that the roughest winds abate with time. Hatred and self-seeking and mischance and, above all, the frailties innate in us--these buffet us for a while, and we are puzzled, and we demand of God, as Job did, why is this permitted? And then as the hair dwindles, the wit grows."

"Oh, yes, with age we take a slackening hold upon events; we let all happenings go by more lightly; and we even concede the universe not to be under any actual bond to be intelligible. Yes, that is true. But is it gain, my poet? for I had thought it to be loss."

"With age we gain the priceless certainty that sorrow and injustice are ephemeral. Solvitur ambulando, my dear. I have attested this merely by living long enough. I, like any other man of my years, have in my day known more or less every grief which the world breeds; and each maddened me in turn, as each was duly salved by time; so that to-day their ravages vex me no more than do the bee-stings I got when I was an urchin. To-day I grant the world to be composed of muck and sunshine intermingled; but, upon the whole, I find the sunshine more pleasant to look at, and--greedily, because my time for sightseeing is not very long--I stare at it. And I hold Judith's creed to be the best of all imaginable creeds--that if we do nothing very wrong, all human imbroglios, in some irrational and quite incomprehensible fashion, will be straightened to our satisfaction. Meanwhile, you also voice a tonic truth--this universe of ours, and, reverently speaking, the Maker of this universe as well, is under no actual bond to be intelligible in dealing with us." He laughed at this season and fell into a lighter tone. "Do I preach like a little conventicle-attending tradesman? Faith, you must remember that when I talk gravely Judith listens as if it were an oracle discoursing. For Judith loves me as the wisest and the best of men. I protest her adoration frightens me. What if she were to find me out?"

"I loved what was divine in you," the woman answered.

"Oddly enough, that is the perfect truth! And when what was divine in me had burned a sufficiency of incense to your vanity, your vanity's owner drove off in a fine coach and left me to die in a garret. Then Judith came. Then Judith nursed and tended and caressed me--and Judith only in all the world!--as once you did that boy you spoke of. Ah, madam, and does not sorrow sometimes lie awake o' nights in the low cradle of that child? and sometimes walk with you by day and clasp your hand--much as his tiny hand did once, so trustingly, so like the clutching of a vine--and beg you never to be friends with anything save sorrow? And do you wholeheartedly love those other women's boys--who did not die? Yes, I remember. Judith, too, remembered. I was her father, for all that I had forsaken my family to dance Jack-pudding attendance on a fine Court lady. So Judith came. And Judith, who sees in play-writing just a very uncertain way of making money--Judith, who cannot tell a B from a bull's foot,--why, Judith, madam, did not ask, but gave, what was divine."

"You are unfair," she cried. "Oh, you are cruel, you juggle words, make knives of them. . . . You" and she spoke as with difficulty--"you have no right to know just how I loved my boy! You should be either man or woman!"

He said pensively: "Yes, I am cruel. But you had mirth and beauty once, and I had only love and a vocabulary. Who then more flagrantly abused the gifts God gave? And why should I not be cruel to you, who made a master-poet of me for your recreation? Lord, what a deal of ruined life it takes to make a little art! Yes, yes, I know. Under old oaks lovers will mouth my verses, and the acorns are not yet shaped from which those oaks will spring. My adoration and your perfidy, all that I have suffered, all that I have failed in even, has gone toward the building of an enduring monument. All these will be immortal, because youth is immortal, and youth delights in demanding explanations of infinity. And only to this end I have suffered and have catalogued the ravings of a perverse disease which has robbed my life of all the normal privileges of life as flame shrivels hair from the arm--that young fools such as I was once might be pleased to murder my rhetoric, and scribblers parody me in their fictions, and schoolboys guess at the date of my death!" This he said with more than ordinary animation; and then he shook his head. "There is a leaven," he said--"there is a leaven even in your smuggest and most inconsiderable tradesman."

She answered, with a wistful smile: "I, too, regret my poet. And just now you are more like him----"

"Faith, but he was really a poet--or, at least, at times----?"

"Not marble, nor the gilded monuments of princes shall outlive this powerful rhyme----'"

"Dear, dear!" he said, in petulant vexation; "how horribly emotion botches verse. That clash of sibilants is both harsh and ungrammatical. **Shall** should be changed to **will**." And at that the woman sighed, because, in common with all persons who never essayed creative verbal composition, she was quite certain per-durable writing must spring from a surcharged heart, rather than from a rearrange-ment of phrases. And so,

"Very unfeignedly I regret my poet," she said, "my poet, who was unhappy and unreasonable, because I was not always wise or kind, or even just. And I did not know until to-day how much I loved my poet. . . . Yes, I know now I loved him. I must go now. I would I had not come."

Then, standing face to face, he cried, "Eh, madam, and what if I also have lied to you--in part? Our work is done; what more is there to say?"

"Nothing," she answered--"nothing. Not even for you, who are a master-smith of words to-day and nothing more."

"I?" he replied. "Do you so little emulate a higher example that even for a mo-ment you consider me?"

She did not answer.

When she had gone, the playmaker sat for a long while in meditation; and then smilingly he took up his pen. He was bound for "an uninhabited island" where all disasters ended in a happy climax.

"So, so!" he was declaiming, later on: "We, too, are kin To dreams and visions; and our little life Is gilded by such faint and cloud-wrapped suns--Only, that needs a homelier touch. Rather, let us say, **We are such stuff As dreams are made on**--Oh, good, good!--Now to pad out the line. . . . In any event, the Bermudas are a seasonable topic. Now here, instead of **thickly-templed India**, suppose we write **the still-vexed Bermoothes**--Good, good! It fits in well enough. . . ."

And so in clerkly fashion he sat about the accomplishment of his stint of labor in time for dinner. A competent workman is not disastrously upset by interruption; and, indeed, he found the notion of surprising Judith with an unlooked-for trinket or so to be at first a very efficacious spur to composition.

And presently the strong joy of creating kindled in him, and phrase flowed abreast with thought, and the playmaker wrote fluently and surely to an accompaniment of contented ejaculations. He regretted nothing, he would not now have laid aside his pen to take up a scepter. For surely--he would have said--to live untroubled, and weave beautiful and winsome dreams is the most desirable of human fates. But he did not consciously think of this, because he was midcourse in the evoking of a mimic tempest which, having purged its victims of unkindliness and error, aimed (in the end) only to sink into an amiable calm.

CONCERNING CORINNA

D r. Herrick told me that, in common with all the Enlightened or Illuminated Brothers, of which prying sect the age breeds so many, he trusted the great lines of Nature, not in the whole, but in part, as they believed Nature was in certain senses not true, and a betrayer, and that she was not wholly the benevolent power to endow, as accorded with the prevailing deceived notion of the vulgar. But he wished not to discuss more particularly than thus, as he had drawn up to himself a certain frontier of reticence; and so fell to petting a great black pig, of which he made an unseemly companion, and to talking idly."

> A Gyges ring they bear about them still,
> To be, and not, seen when and where they will;
>
> They tread on clouds, and though they sometimes fall,
> They fall like dew, and make no noise at all:
>
> So silently they one to th' other come
> As colors steal into the pear or plum;
>
> And air-like, leave no pression to be seen
> Where'er they met, or parting place has been.
>
> ROBERT HERRICK.--My Lovers how They Come and Part.

CONCERNING CORINNA

The matter hinges entirely upon whether or not Robert Herrick was insane. Sir Thomas Browne always preferred to think that he was; whereas Philip Borsdale perversely considered the answer to be optional. Perversely, Sir Thomas protested, because he said that to believe in Herrick's sanity was not conducive to your own.

This much is certain: the old clergyman, a man of few friends and no intimates, enjoyed in Devon, thanks to his time-hallowed reputation for singularity, a certain immunity. In and about Dean Prior, for instance, it was conceded in 1674 that it was unusual for a divine of the Church of England to make a black pig--and a pig of peculiarly diabolical ugliness, at that--his ordinary associate; but Dean Prior had come long ago to accept the grisly brute as a concomitant of Dr. Herrick's presence almost as inevitable as his shadow. It was no crime to be fond of dumb animals, not even of one so inordinately unprepossessing; and you allowed for eccentricities, in any event, in dealing with a poet.

For Totnes, Buckfastleigh, Dean Prior--all that part of Devon, in fact--complacently basked in the reflected glory of Robert Herrick. People came from a long distance, now that the Parliamentary Wars were over, in order just to see the writer of the *Hesperides* and the *Noble Numbers*. And such enthusiasts found in Robert Herrick a hideous dreamy man, who, without ever perpetrating any actual discourtesy, always managed to dismiss them, somehow, with a sense of having been rebuffed.

Sir Thomas Browne, that ardent amateur of the curious, came into Devon, however, without the risk of incurring any such fate, inasmuch as the knight traveled westward simply to discuss with Master Philip Borsdale the recent doings of Cardinal Alioneri. Now, Philip Borsdale, as Sir Thomas knew, had been employed by Herrick in various transactions here irrelevant. In consequence, Sir Thomas Browne was not greatly surprised when, on his arrival at Buckfastleigh, Borsdale's body-servant told him that Master Borsdale had left instructions for Sir Thomas to follow him to Dean Prior. Browne complied, because his business with Borsdale was of importance.

Philip Borsdale was lounging in Dr. Herrick's chair, intent upon a lengthy manuscript, alone and to all appearances quite at home. The state of the room Sir Thomas found extraordinary; but he had graver matters to discuss; and he explained the results of his mission without extraneous comment.

"Yes, you have managed it to admiration," said Philip Borsdale, when the knight had made an end. Borsdale leaned back and laughed, purringly, for the outcome of this affair of the Cardinal and the Wax Image meant much to him from a pecuniary standpoint. "Yet it is odd a prince of any church which has done so much toward the discomfiture of sorcery should have entertained such ideas. It is also odd to note the series of coincidences which appears to have attended this Alioneri's practises."

"I noticed that," said Sir Thomas. After a while he said: "You think, then, that they must have been coincidences?"

"MUST is a word which intelligent people do not outwear by too constant usage."

And "Oh----?" said the knight, and said that alone, because he was familiar with the sparkle now in Borsdale's eyes, and knew it heralded an adventure for an amateur of the curious.

"I am not committing myself, mark you, Sir Thomas, to any statement whatever, beyond the observation that these coincidences were noticeable. I add, with superficial irrelevance, that Dr. Herrick disappeared last night."

"I am not surprised," said Sir Thomas, drily. "No possible antics would astonish me on the part of that unvenerable madman. When I was last in Totnes, he broke down in the midst of a sermon, and flung the manuscript of it at his congregation, and cursed them roundly for not paying closer attention. Such was never my ideal of absolute decorum in the pulpit. Moreover, it is unusual for a minister of the Church of England to be accompanied everywhere by a pig with whom he discusses the affairs of the parish precisely as if the pig were a human being."

"The pig--he whimsically called the pig Corinna, sir, in honor of that imaginary mistress to whom he addressed so many verses--why, the pig also has disappeared. Oh, but of course that at least is simply a coincidence. . . . I grant you it was an uncanny beast. And I grant you that Dr. Herrick was a dubious ornament to his calling. Of that I am doubly certain to-day," said Borsdale, and he waved his hand comprehensively, "in view of the state in which--you see--he left this room. Yes, he was quietly writing here at eleven o'clock last night when old Prudence Baldwin, his housekeeper, last saw him. Afterward Dr. Herrick appears to have diverted himself by taking away the mats and chalking geometrical designs upon the floor, as well as by burning some sort of incense in this brasier."

"But such avocations, Philip, are not necessarily indicative of sanity. No, it is not, upon the whole, an inevitable manner for an elderly parson to while away an evening."

"Oh, but that was only a part, sir. He also left the clothes he was wearing--in a rather peculiarly constructed heap, as you can see. Among them, by the way, I found this flattened and corroded bullet. That puzzled me. I think I understand it now." Thus Borsdale, as he composedly smoked his churchwarden. "In short, the whole affair is as mysterious----"

Here Sir Thomas raised his hand. "Spare me the simile. I detect a vista of curious perils such as infinitely outshines verbal brilliancy. You need my aid in some insane attempt." He considered. He said: "So! you have been retained?"

"I have been asked to help him. Of course I did not know of what he meant to try. In short, Dr. Herrick left this manuscript, as well as certain instructions for me. The last are--well! unusual."

"Ah, yes! You hearten me. I have long had my suspicions as to this Herrick, though. . . . And what are we to do?"

"I really cannot inform you, sir. I doubt if I could explain in any workaday English even what we will attempt to do," said Philip Borsdale. "I do say this: You believe the business which we have settled, involving as it does the lives of thousands of men and women, to be of importance. I swear to you that, as set against what we will essay, all we have done is trivial. As pitted against the business we will attempt to-night, our previous achievements are suggestive of the evolutions of two sand-fleas beside the ocean. The prize at which this adventure aims is so stupendous that I cannot name it."

"Oh, but you must, Philip. I am no more afraid of the local constabulary than I am of the local notions as to what respectability entails. I may confess, however, that I am afraid of wagering against unknown odds."

Borsdale reflected. Then he said, with deliberation: "Dr. Herrick's was, when you come to think of it, an unusual life. He is--or perhaps I ought to say he was--upward of eighty-three. He has lived here for over a half-century, and during that time he has never attempted to make either a friend or an enemy. He was--indifferent, let us say. Talking to Dr. Herrick was, somehow, like talking to a man in a fog. . . . Meanwhile, he wrote his verses to imaginary women--to Corinna and Julia, to Myrha, Electra and Perilla--those lovely, shadow women who never, in so far as we know, had any real existence----"

Sir Thomas smiled. "Of course. They are mere figments of the poet, pegs to hang rhymes on. And yet--let us go on. I know that Herrick never willingly so much as spoke with a woman."

"Not in so far as we know, I said." And Borsdale paused. "Then, too, he wrote such dainty, merry poems about the fairies. Yes, it was all of fifty years ago that Dr. Herrick first appeared in print with his **Description of the King and Queen of the Fairies**. The thought seems always to have haunted him."

The knight's face changed, a little by a little. "I have long been an amateur of the curious," he said, strangely quiet. "I do not think that anything you may say will surprise me inordinately."

"He had found in every country in the world traditions of a race who were human--yet more than human. That is the most exact fashion in which I can express his beginnings. On every side he found the notion of a race who can impinge on mortal life and partake of it--but always without exercising the last reach of their endowments. Oh, the tradition exists everywhere, whether you call these occasional interlopers fauns, fairies, gnomes, ondines, incubi, or demons. They could, according to these fables, temporarily restrict themselves into our life, just as a swimmer may elect to use only one arm--or, a more fitting comparison, become apparent to our human senses in the fashion of a cube which can obtrude only one of its six surfaces into a plane. You follow me, of course, sir?--to the triangles and circles and hexagons this cube would seem to be an ordinary square. Conceiving such a race to exist, we might talk with them, might jostle them in the streets, might even intermarry with them, sir--and always see in them only human beings, and solely because of our senses' limitations."

"I comprehend. These are exactly the speculations that would appeal to an unbalanced mind--is that not your thought, Philip?"

"Why, there is nothing particularly insane, Sir Thomas, in desiring to explore in fields beyond those which our senses make perceptible. It is very certain these fields exist; and the question of their extent I take to be both interesting and important."

Then Sir Thomas said: "Like any other rational man, I have occasionally thought of this endeavor at which you hint. We exist--you and I and all the others--in what we glibly call the universe. All that we know of it is through what we entitle our five senses, which, when provoked to action, will cause a chemical change in a few ounces of spongy matter packed in our skulls. There are no grounds for believing that this particular method of communication is adequate, or even that the agents which produce it are veracious. Meanwhile, we are in touch with what exists through our five senses only. It may be that they lie to us. There is, at least, no reason for assuming them to be infallible."

"But reflection plows a deeper furrow, Sir Thomas. Even in the exercise of any one of these five senses it is certain that we are excelled by what we vaingloriously call the lower forms of life. A dog has powers of scent we cannot reach to, birds hear the crawling of a worm, insects distinguish those rays in the spectrum which lie beyond violet and red, and are invisible to us; and snails and fish and ants--perhaps all other living creatures, indeed--have senses which man does not share at all, and has no name for. Granted that we human beings alone possess the power of reasoning, the fact remains that we invariably start with false premises, and always pass our judgments when biased at the best by incomplete reports of everything in the universe, and very possibly by reports which lie flat-footedly."

You saw that Browne was troubled. Now he rose. "Nothing will come of this. I do not touch upon the desirability of conquering those fields at which we dare only to hint. No, I am not afraid. I dare assist you in doing anything Dr. Herrick asks, because I know that nothing will come of such endeavors. Much is permitted us--'but of the fruit of the tree which is in the midst of the garden, God hath said, to us who are no more than human, Ye shall not eat of it.'"

"Yet Dr. Herrick, as many other men have done, thought otherwise. I, too, will venture a quotation. 'Didst thou never see a lark in a cage? Such is the soul in the body: this world is like her little turf of grass, and the heavens o'er our heads, like her looking-glass, only gives us a miserable knowledge of the small compass of our prison.' Many years ago that lamentation was familiar. What wonder, then, that Dr. Herrick should have dared to repeat it yesterday? And what wonder if he tried to free the prisoner?"

"Such freedom is forbidden," Sir Thomas stubbornly replied. "I have long known that Herrick was formerly in correspondence with John Heydon, and Robert Flood, and others of the Illuminated, as they call themselves. There are many of this sect in England, as we all know; and we hear much silly chatter of Elixirs and Philosopher's Stones in connection with them. But I happen to know somewhat of their real aims and tenets. I do not care to know any more than I do. If it be true that all of which man is conscious is just a portion of a curtain, and that the actual universe in nothing resembles our notion of it, I am willing to believe this curtain was placed there for some righteous and wise reason. They tell me the curtain may be lifted. Whether this be true or no, I must for my own sanity's sake insist it can never be lifted."

"But what if it were not forbidden? For Dr. Herrick asserts he has already demonstrated that."

Sir Thomas interrupted, with odd quickness. "True, we must bear it in mind the man never married--Did he, by any chance, possess a crystal of Venice glass three inches square?"

And Borsdale gaped. "I found it with his manuscript. But he said nothing of it. . . . How could you guess?"

Sir Thomas reflectively scraped the edge of the glass with his finger-nail. "You would be none the happier for knowing, Philip. Yes, that is a blood-stain here. I see. And Herrick, so far as we know, had never in his life loved any woman. He is the only poet in history who never demonstrably loved any woman. I think you had better read me his manuscript, Philip."

This Philip Borsdale did.

Then Sir Thomas said, as quiet epilogue: "This, if it be true, would explain much as to that lovely land of eternal spring and daffodils and friendly girls, of which his verses make us free. It would even explain Corinna and Herrick's rapt living without any human ties. For all poets since the time of AEschylus, who could not write until he was too drunken to walk, have been most readily seduced by whatever stimulus most tended to heighten their imaginings; so that for the sake of a song's perfection they have freely resorted to divers artificial inspirations, and very often without evincing any undue squeamishness. . . . I spoke of AEschylus. I am sorry, Philip, that you are not familiar with ancient Greek life. There is so much I could tell you of, in that event, of the quaint cult of Kore, or Pherephatta, and of the swine of Eubouleus, and of certain ambiguous maidens, whom those old Grecians fabled--oh, very ignorantly fabled, my lad, of course--to rule in a more quietly lit and more tranquil world than we blunder about. I think I could explain much which now seems mysterious--yes, and the daffodils, also, that Herrick wrote of so constantly. But it is better not to talk of these sinister delusions of heathenry." Sir Thomas shrugged. "For my reward would be to have you think me mad. I prefer to iterate the verdict of all logical people, and formally to register my opinion that Robert Herrick was indisputably a lunatic."

Borsdale did not seem perturbed. "I think the record of his experiments is true, in any event. You will concede that their results were startling? And what if his deductions be the truth? what if our limited senses have reported to us so very little of the universe, and even that little untruthfully?" He laughed and drummed impatiently upon the table. "At least, he tells us that the boy returned. I fervently believe that in this matter Dr. Herrick was capable of any crime except falsehood. Oh, no I depend on it, he also will return."

"You imagine Herrick will break down the door between this world and that other inconceivable world which all of us have dreamed of! To me, my lad, it seems as if this Herrick aimed dangerously near to repetition of the Primal Sin, for all that he handles it like a problem in mechanical mathematics. The poet writes as if he were instructing a dame's school as to the advisability of becoming omnipotent."

"Well, well! I am not defending Dr. Herrick in anything save his desire to know the truth. In this respect at least, he has proven himself to be both admirable and fearless. And at worst, he only strives to do what Jacob did at Peniel," said Philip Borsdale, lightly. "The patriarch, as I recall, was blessed for acting as he did. The legend is not irrelevant, I think."

They passed into the adjoining room.

Thus the two men came into a high-ceiled apartment, cylindrical in shape, with plastered walls painted green everywhere save for the quaint embellishment of a large oval, wherein a woman, having an eagle's beak, grasped in one hand a serpent and in the other a knife. Sir Thomas Browne seemed to recognize this curious design, and gave an ominous nod.

Borsdale said: "You see Dr. Herrick had prepared everything. And much of what we are about to do is merely symbolical, of course. Most people undervalue symbols. They do not seem to understand that there could never have been any conceivable need of inventing a periphrasis for what did not exist."

Sir Thomas Browne regarded Borsdale for a while intently. Then the knight gave his habitual shrugging gesture. "You are braver than I, Philip, because you are more ignorant than I. I have been too long an amateur of the curious. Sometimes in over-credulous moments I have almost believed that in sober verity there are reasoning beings who are not human--beings that for their own dark purposes seek union with us. Indeed, I went into Pomerania once to talk with John Dietrick of Ramdin. He told me one of those relations whose truth we dread, a tale which I did not dare, I tell you candidly, even to discuss in my *Vulgar Errors*. Then there is Helgi Thorison's history, and that of Leonard of Basle also. Oh, there are more recorded stories of this nature than you dream of, Philip. We have only the choice between believing that all these men were madmen, and believing that ordinary human life is led by a drugged animal who drowses through a purblind existence among merciful veils. And these female creatures--these Corinnas, Perillas, Myrhas, and Electras--can it be possible that they are always striving, for their own strange ends, to rouse the sleeping animal and break the kindly veils?--and are they permitted to use such amiable enticements as Herrick describes? Oh, no, all this is just a madman's dream, dear lad, and we must not dare to consider it seriously, lest we become no more sane than he."

"But you will aid me?" Borsdale said.

"Yes, I will aid you, Philip, for in Herrick's case I take it that the mischief is consummated already; and we, I think, risk nothing worse than death. But you will need another knife a little later--a knife that will be clean."

"I had forgotten." Borsdale withdrew, and presently returned with a bone-handled knife. And then he made a light. "Are you quite ready, sir?"

Sir Thomas Browne, that aging amateur of the curious, could not resist a laugh.

And then they sat about proceedings of which, for obvious reasons, the details are best left unrecorded. It was not an unconscionable while before they seemed to be aware of unusual phenomena. But as Sir Thomas always pointed out, in subsequent discussions, these were quite possibly the fruitage of excited imagination.

"Now, Philip!--now, give me the knife!" cried Sir Thomas Browne. He knew for the first time, despite many previous mischancy happenings, what real terror was.

The room was thick with blinding smoke by this, so that Borsdale could see nothing save his co-partner in this adventure. Both men were shaken by what had occurred before. Borsdale incuriously perceived that old Sir Thomas rose, tense as a cat about to pounce, and that he caught the unstained knife from Borsdale's hand, and flung it like a javelin into the vapor which encompassed them. This gesture stirred the smoke so that Borsdale could see the knife quiver and fall, and note the tiny triangle of unbared plaster it had cut in the painted woman's breast. Within the same instant he had perceived a naked man who staggered.

"Iz adu kronyeshnago----!" The intruder's thin, shrill wail was that of a frightened child. The man strode forward, choked, seemed to grope his way. His face was not good to look at. Horror gripped and tore at every member of the cadaverous old body, as a high wind tugs at a flag. The two witnesses of Herrick's agony did not stir during the instant wherein the frenzied man stooped, moving stiffly like an ill-made toy, and took up the knife.

"Oh, yes, I knew what he was about to do," said Sir Thomas Browne afterward, in his quiet fashion. "I did not try to stop him. If Herrick had been my dearest friend, I would not have interfered. I had seen his face, you comprehend. Yes, it was kinder to let him die. It was curious, though, as he stood there hacking his chest, how at each stab he deliberately twisted the knife. I suppose the pain distracted his mind from what he was remembering. I should have forewarned Borsdale of this possible outcome at the very first, I suppose. But, then, which one of us is always wise?"

So this adventure came to nothing. For its significance, if any, hinged upon Robert Herrick's sanity, which was at best a disputable quantity. Grant him insane, and the whole business, as Sir Thomas was at large pains to point out, dwindles at once into the irresponsible vagaries of a madman.

"And all the while, for what we know, he had been hiding somewhere in the house. We never searched it. Oh, yes, there is no doubt he was insane," said Sir Thomas, comfortably.

"Faith! what he moaned was gibberish, of course----"

"Oddly enough, his words were intelligible. They meant in Russian 'Out of the lowest hell.'"

"But, why, in God's name, Russian?"

"I am sure I do not know," Sir Thomas replied; and he did not appear at all to regret his ignorance.

But Borsdale meditated, disappointedly. "Oh, yes, the outcome is ambiguous, Sir Thomas, in every way. I think we may safely take it as a warning, in any event, that this world of ours, whatever its deficiencies, was meant to be inhabited by men and women only."

"Now I," was Sir Thomas's verdict, "prefer to take it as a warning that insane people ought to be restrained."

"Ah, well, insanity is only one of the many forms of being abnormal. Yes, I think it proves that all abnormal people ought to be restrained. Perhaps it proves that they are very potently restrained," said Philip Borsdale, perversely.

Perversely, Sir Thomas always steadfastly protested, because he said that to believe in Herrick's sanity was not conducive to your own.

So Sir Thomas shrugged, and went toward the open window. Without the road was a dazzling gray under the noon sun, for the sky was cloudless. The ordered trees were rustling pleasantly, very brave in their autumnal liveries. Under a maple across the way some seven laborers were joking lazily as they ate their dinner. A wagon lumbered by, the driver whistling. In front of the house a woman had stopped to rearrange the pink cap of the baby she was carrying. The child had just reached up fat and uncertain little arms to kiss her. Nothing that Browne saw was out of ordinary, kindly human life.

"Well, after all," said Sir Thomas, upon a sudden, "for one, I think it is an endurable world, just as it stands."

And Borsdale looked up from a letter he had been reading. It was from a woman who has no concern with this tale, and its contents were of no importance to any one save Borsdale.

"Now, do you know," said Philip Borsdale, "I am beginning to think you the most sensible man of my acquaintance! Oh, yes, beyond doubt it is an endurable sun-nurtured world--just as it stands. It makes it doubly odd that Dr. Herrick should have chosen always to

'Write of groves, and twilights, and to sing The court of Mab, and of the Fairy King, And write of Hell.'"

Sir Thomas touched his arm, protestingly. "Ah, but you have forgotten what follows, Philip--

'I sing, and ever shall, Of Heaven,--and hope to have it after all.'"

"Well! I cry Amen," said Borsdale. "But I wish I could forget the old man's face."

"Oh, and I also," Sir Thomas said. "And I cry Amen with far more heartiness, my lad, because I, too, once dreamed of--of Corinna, shall we say?"

OLIVIA'S POTTAGE

Mr. Wycherley was naturally modest until King Charles' court, that late disgrace to our times, corrupted him. He then gave himself up to all sorts of extravagances and to the wildest frolics that a wanton wit could devise. . . . Never was so much ill-nature in a pen as in his, joined with so much good nature as was in himself, even to excess; for he was bountiful, even to run himself into difficulties, and charitable even to a fault. It was not that he was free from the failings of humanity, but he had the tenderness of it, too, which made everybody excuse whom everybody loved; and even the asperity of his verses seems to have been forgiven."

I the Plain Dealer am to act to-day.

Now, you shrewd judges, who the boxes sway,
Leading the ladies' hearts and sense astray,
And for their sakes, see all and hear no play;
Correct your cravats, foretops, lock behind:
The dress and breeding of the play ne'er mind;
For the coarse dauber of the coming scenes
To follow life and nature only means,
Displays you as you are, makes his fine woman
A mercenary jilt and true to no man,
Shows men of wit and pleasure of the age
Are as dull rogues as ever cumber'd stage.

WILLIAM WYCHERLEY.--Prologue to The Plain Dealer.

OLIVIA'S POTTAGE

It was in the May of 1680 that Mr. William Wycherley went into the country to marry the famed heiress, Mistress Araminta Vining, as he had previously settled with her father, and found her to his vast relief a very personable girl. She had in consequence a host of admirers, pre-eminent among whom was young Robert Minifie of Milanor. Mr. Wycherley, a noted stickler for etiquette, decorously made bold to question Mr. Minifie's taste in a dispute concerning waistcoats. A duel was decorously arranged and these two met upon the narrow beach of Teviot Bay.

Theirs was a spirited encounter, lasting for ten energetic minutes. Then Wycherley pinked Mr. Minifie in the shoulder, just as the dramatist, a favorite pupil of Gerard's, had planned to do; and the four gentlemen parted with every imaginable courtesy, since the wounded man and the two seconds were to return by boat to Mr. Minifie's house at Milanor.

More lately Wycherley walked in the direction of Ouseley Manor, whistling *Love's a Toy*. Honor was satisfied, and, happily, as he reflected, at no expense of life. He was a kindly hearted fop, and more than once had killed his man with perfectly sincere regret. But in putting on his coat--it was the black camlet coat with silver buttons--he had overlooked his sleevelinks; and he did not recognize, for twenty-four eventful hours, the full importance of his carelessness.

In the heart of Figgis Wood, the incomparable Countess of Drogheda, aunt to Mr. Wycherley's betrothed, and a noted leader of fashion, had presently paused at sight of him--laughing a little--and with one tiny hand had made as though to thrust back the staghound which accompanied her. "Your humble servant, Mr. Swashbuckler," she said; and then: "But oh! you have not hurt the lad?" she demanded, with a tincture of anxiety.

"Nay, after a short but brilliant engagement," Wycherley returned, "Mr. Minifie was very harmlessly perforated; and in consequence I look to be married on Thursday, after all."

"Let me die but Cupid never meets with anything save inhospitality in this gross world!" cried Lady Drogheda. "For the boy is heels over head in love with

Araminta,--oh, a second Almanzor! And my niece does not precisely hate him either, let me tell you, William, for all your month's assault of essences and perfumed gloves and apricot paste and other small artillery of courtship. La, my dear, was it only a month ago we settled your future over a couple of Naples biscuit and a bottle of Rhenish?" She walked beside him now, and the progress of these exquisites was leisurely. There were many trees at hand so huge as to necessitate a considerable detour.

"Egad, it is a month and three days over," Wycherley retorted, "since you suggested your respected brother-in-law was ready to pay my debts in full, upon condition I retaliated by making your adorable niece Mistress Wycherley. Well, I stand to-day indebted to him for an advance of L1500 and am no more afraid of bailiffs. We have performed a very creditable stroke of business; and the day after to-morrow you will have fairly earned your L500 for arranging the marriage. Faith, and in earnest of this, I already begin to view you through appropriate lenses as undoubtedly the most desirable aunt in the universe."

Nor was there any unconscionable stretching of the phrase. Through the quiet forest, untouched as yet by any fidgeting culture, and much as it was when John Lackland wooed Hawisa under, its venerable oaks, old even then, the little widow moved like a light flame. She was clothed throughout in scarlet, after her high-hearted style of dress, and carried a tall staff of ebony; and the gold head of it was farther from the dead leaves than was her mischievous countenance. The big staghound lounged beside her. She pleased the eye, at least, did this heartless, merry and selfish Olivia, whom Wycherley had so ruthlessly depicted in his ***Plain Dealer***. To the last detail Wycherley found her, as he phrased it, "mignonne et piquante," and he told her so.

Lady Drogheda observed, "Fiddle-de-dee!" Lady Drogheda continued: "Yes, I am a fool, of course, but then I still remember Bessington, and the boy that went mad there----"

"Because of a surfeit of those dreams 'such as the poets know when they are young.' Sweet chuck, beat not the bones of the buried; when he breathed he was a likely lad," Mr. Wycherley declared, with signal gravity.

"Oh, la, la!" she flouted him. "Well, in any event you were the first gentleman in England to wear a neckcloth of Flanders lace."

"And you were the first person of quality to eat cheesecakes in Spring Garden," he not half so mirthfully retorted. "So we have not entirely failed in life, it may be, after all."

She made of him a quite irrelevant demand: "D'ye fancy Esau was contented, William?"

"I fancy he was fond of pottage, madam; and that, as I remember, he got his pottage. Come, now, a tangible bowl of pottage, piping hot, is not to be despised in such a hazardous world as ours is."

She was silent for a lengthy while. "Lord, Lord, how musty all that brave, sweet nonsense seems!" she said, and almost sighed. "Eh, well! *le vin est tire, et il faut le boire*."

"My adorable aunt! Let us put it a thought less dumpishly; and render thanks because our pottage smokes upon the table, and we are blessed with excellent appetites."

"So that in a month we will be back again in the playhouses and Hyde Park and Mulberry Garden, or nodding to each other in the New Exchange,--you with your debts paid, and I with my L500----?" She paused to pat the staghound's head. "Lord Remon came this afternoon," said Lady Drogheda, and with averted eyes.

"I do not approve of Remon," he announced. "Nay, madam, even a Siren ought to spare her kin and show some mercy toward the more stagnant-blooded fish."

And Lady Drogheda shrugged. "He is very wealthy, and I am lamentably poor. One must not seek noon at fourteen o'clock or clamor for better bread than was ever made from wheat."

Mr. Wycherley laughed, after a pregnant silence.

"By heavens, madam, you are in the right! So I shall walk no more in Figgis Wood, for its old magic breeds too many day-dreams. Besides, we have been serious for half-an-hour. Now, then, let us discuss theology, dear aunt, or millinery, or metaphysics, or the King's new statue at Windsor, or, if you will, the last Spring Garden scandal. Or let us count the leaves upon this tree; and afterward I will enumerate my reasons for believing yonder crescent moon to be the paring of the Angel Gabriel's left thumb-nail."

She was a woman of eloquent silences when there was any need of them; and thus the fop and the coquette traversed the remainder of that solemn wood without any further speech. Modish people would have esteemed them unwontedly glum.

Wycherley discovered in a while the absence of his sleeve-links, and was properly vexed by the loss of these not unhandsome trinkets, the gifts of Lady Castlemaine in the old days when Mr. Wycherley was the King's successful rival for her favors. But Wycherley knew the tide filled Teviot Bay and wondering fishes were at liberty to muzzle the toys, by this, and merely shrugged at his mishap, midcourse in toilet.

Mr. Wycherley, upon mature deliberation, wore the green suit with yellow ribbons, since there was a ball that night in honor of his nearing marriage, and a confluence of gentry to attend it. Miss Vining and he walked through a minuet to some applause; the two were heartily acclaimed a striking couple, and congratulations beat about their ears as thick as sugar-plums in a carnival. And at nine you might have found the handsome dramatist alone upon the East Terrace of Ouseley, pacing to and fro in the moonlight, and complacently reflecting upon his quite indisputable and, past doubt, unmerited good fortune.

There was never any night in June which nature planned the more adroitly. Soft and warm and windless, lit by a vainglorious moon and every star that ever shone, the beauty of this world caressed and heartened its beholder like a gallant music. Our universe, Mr. Wycherley conceded willingly, was excellent and kindly, and the Arbiter of it too generous; for here was he, the wastrel, like the third prince at the end of a fairy-tale, the master of a handsome wife, and a fine house and fortune. Somewhere, he knew, young Minifie, with his arm in a sling, was pleading with Mistress Araminta for the last time; and this reflection did not greatly trouble Mr. Wycherley, since incommunicably it tickled his vanity. He was chuckling when he came to the open window.

Within a woman was singing, to the tinkling accompaniment of a spinet, for the delectation of Lord Remon. She was not uncomely, and the hard, lean, stingy countenance of the attendant nobleman was almost genial. Wycherley understood with a great rending shock, as though the thought were novel, that Olivia, Lady Drogheda, designed to marry this man, who grinned within finger's reach--or, rather, to ally herself with Remon's inordinate wealth,--and without any heralding a brutal rage and hatred of all created things possessed the involuntary eavesdropper.

She looked up into Remon's face and, laughing with such bright and elfin mirth as never any other woman showed, thought Wycherley, she broke into another song. She would have spared Mr. Wycherley that had she but known him to be within earshot. . . . Oh, it was only Lady Drogheda who sang, he knew,--the seasoned gamester and coquette, the veteran of London and of Cheltenham,--but the woman had no right to charm this haggler with a voice that was not hers. For it was the voice of another Olivia, who was not a fine and urban lady, and who lived nowhere any longer; it was the voice of a soft-handed, tender, jeering girl, whom he alone remembered; and a sick, illimitable rage grilled in each vein of him as liltingly she sang, for Remon, the old and foolish song which Wycherley had made in her praise very long ago, and of which he might not ever forget the most trivial word.

Men, even beaux, are strangely constituted; and so it needed only this--the sudden stark brute jealousy of one male animal for another. That was the clumsy hand which now unlocked the dyke; and like a flood, tall and resistless, came the recollection of their far-off past and of its least dear trifle, of all the aspirations and absurdities and splendors of their common youth, and found him in its path, a painted fellow, a spendthrift king of the mode, a most notable authority upon the set of a peruke, a penniless, spent connoisseur of stockings, essences and cosmetics.

He got but little rest this night.

There were too many plaintive memories which tediously plucked him back, with feeble and innumerable hands, as often as he trod upon the threshold of sleep. Then too, there were so many dreams, half-waking, and not only of Olivia Chichele, naive and frank in divers rural circumstances, but rather of Olivia, Lady Drogheda, that perfect piece of artifice; of how exquisite she was! how swift and volatile in every movement! how airily indomitable, and how mendacious to the tips of her polished finger-nails! and how she always seemed to flit about this world as joyously, alertly, and as colorfully as some ornate and tiny bird of the tropics!

But presently parochial birds were wrangling underneath the dramatist's window, while he tossed and assured himself that he was sleepier than any saint who ever snored in Ephesus; and presently one hand of Moncrieff was drawing the bed-curtains, while the other carefully balanced a mug of shaving-water.

Wycherley did not see her all that morning, for Lady Drogheda was fatigued, or so a lackey informed him, and as yet kept her chamber. His Araminta he found deplorably sullen. So the dramatist devoted the better part of this day to a refitting of his wedding-suit, just come from London; for Moncrieff, an invaluable man, had adjudged the pockets to be placed too high; and, be the punishment deserved or no, Mr. Wycherley had never heard that any victim of law appeared the more admirable upon his scaffold for being slovenly in his attire.

Thus it was as late as five in the afternoon that, wearing the peach-colored suit trimmed with scarlet ribbon, and a new French beaver, the exquisite came upon Lady Drogheda walking in the gardens with only an appropriate peacock for company. She was so beautiful and brilliant and so little--so like a famous gem too suddenly disclosed, and therefore oddly disparate in all these qualities, that his decorous pleasant voice might quite permissibly have shaken a trifle (as indeed it did), when Mr. Wycherley implored Lady Drogheda to walk with him to Teviot Bay, on the off-chance of recovering his sleeve-links.

And there they did find one of the trinkets, but the tide had swept away the other, or else the sand had buried it. So they rested there upon the rocks, after an unavailing search, and talked of many trifles, amid surroundings oddly incongruous.

For this Teviot Bay is a primeval place, a deep-cut, narrow notch in the tip of Carnrick, and is walled by cliffs so high and so precipitous that they exclude a view of anything except the ocean. The bay opens due west; and its white barriers were now developing a violet tinge, for this was on a sullen afternoon, and the sea was ruffled by spiteful gusts. Wycherley could find no color anywhere save in this glowing, tiny and exquisite woman; and everywhere was a gigantic peace, vexed only when high overhead a sea-fowl jeered at these modish persons, as he flapped toward an impregnable nest.

"And by this hour to-morrow," thought Mr. Wycherley, "I shall be chained to that good, strapping, wholesome Juno of a girl!"

So he fell presently into a silence, staring at the vacant west, which was like a huge and sickly pearl, not thinking of anything at all, but longing poignantly for something which was very beautiful and strange and quite unattainable, with precisely that anguish he had sometimes known in awaking from a dream of which he could remember nothing save its piercing loveliness.

"And thus ends the last day of our bachelorhood!" said Lady Drogheda, upon a sudden. "You have played long enough--La, William, you have led the fashion for ten years, you have written four merry comedies, and you have laughed as much as any man alive, but you have pulled down all that nature raised in you, I think. Was it worth while?"

"Faith, but nature's monuments are no longer the last cry in architecture," he replied; "and I believe that *The Plain Dealer* and *The Country Wife* will hold their own."

"And you wrote them when you were just a boy! Ah, yes, you might have been our English Moliere, my dear. And, instead, you have elected to become an authority upon cravats and waistcoats."

"Eh, madam"--he smiled--"there was a time when I too was foolishly intent to divert the leisure hours of posterity. But reflection assured me that posterity had, thus far, done very little to place me under that or any other obligation. Ah, no! Youth, health and--though I say it--a modicum of intelligence are loaned to most of us for a while, and for a terribly brief while. They are but loans, and Time is waiting greedily to snatch them from us. For the perturbed usurer knows that he is lending us, perforce, three priceless possessions, and that till our lease runs out we are free to dispose of them as we elect. Now, had I jealously devoted my allotment of these treasures toward securing for my impressions of the universe a place in yet unprinted libraries, I would have made an investment from which I could not possibly have derived any pleasure, and which would have been to other people of rather dubious benefit. In consequence, I chose a wiser and devouter course."

This statement Lady Drogheda afforded the commentary of a grimace.

"Why, look you," Wycherley philosophized, "have you never thought what a vast deal of loving and painstaking labor must have gone to make the world we inhabit so beautiful and so complete? For it was not enough to evolve and set a glaring sun in heaven, to marshal the big stars about the summer sky, but even in the least frequented meadow every butterfly must have his pinions jeweled, very carefully, and every lovely blade of grass be fashioned separately. The hand that yesterday arranged the Himalayas found time to glaze the wings of a midge! Now, most of us could design a striking Flood, or even a Last judgment, since the canvas is so big and the colors used so virulent; but to paint a snuff-box perfectly you must love the labor for its own sake, and pursue it without even an underthought of the performance's ultimate appraisement. People do not often consider the simple fact that it is enough to bait, and quite superfluous to veneer, a trap; indeed, those generally acclaimed the best of persons insist this world is but an antechamber, full of gins and pitfalls, which must be scurried through with shut eyes. And the more fools they, as all we poets know! for to enjoy a sunset, or a glass of wine, or even to admire the charms of a handsome woman, is to render the Artificer of all at least the tribute of appreciation."

But she said, in a sharp voice: "William, William----!" And he saw that there was no beach now in Teviot Bay except the dwindling crescent at its farthest indentation on which they sat.

Yet his watch, on consultation, recorded only five o'clock; and presently Mr. Wycherley laughed, not very loudly. The two had risen, and her face was a tiny snowdrift where every touch of rouge and grease-pencils showed crudely.

"Look now," said Wycherley, "upon what trifles our lives hinge! Last night I heard you singing, and the song brought back so many things done long ago, and made me so unhappy that--ridiculous conclusion!--I forgot to wind my watch. Well! the tide is buffeting at either side of Carnrick; within the hour this place will be submerged; and, in a phrase, we are as dead as Hannibal or Hector."

She said, very quiet: "Could you not gain the mainland if you stripped and swam for it?"

"Why, possibly," the beau conceded. "Meanwhile you would have drowned. Faith, we had as well make the best of it."

Little Lady Drogheda touched his sleeve, and her hand (as the man noted) did not shake at all, nor did her delicious piping voice shake either. "You cannot save me. I know it. I am not frightened. I bid you save yourself."

"Permit me to assist you to that ledge of rock," Mr. Wycherley answered, "which is a trifle higher than the beach; and I pray you, Olivia, do not mar the dignity of these last passages by talking nonsense."

For he had spied a ledge, not inaccessible, some four feet higher than the sands, and it offered them at least a respite. And within the moment they had secured this niggardly concession, intent to die, as Wycherley observed, like hurt mice upon a pantry-shelf. The business smacked of disproportion, he considered, although too well-bred to say as much; for here was a big ruthless league betwixt earth and sea, and with no loftier end than to crush a fop and a coquette, whose speedier extinction had been dear at the expense of a shilling's worth of arsenic!

Then the sun came out, to peep at these trapped, comely people, and doubtless to get appropriate mirth at the spectacle. He hung low against the misty sky, a clearly-rounded orb that did not dazzle, but merely shone with the cold glitter of new snow upon a fair December day; and for the rest, the rocks, and watery heavens, and all these treacherous and lapping waves, were very like a crude draught of the world, dashed off conceivably upon the day before creation.

These arbiters of social London did not speak at all; and the bleak waters crowded toward them as in a fretful dispute of precedence.

Then the woman said: "Last night Lord Remon asked me to marry him, and I declined the honor. For this place is too like Bessington--and, I think, the past month has changed everything----"

"I thought you had forgotten Bessington," he said, "long, long ago."

"I did not ever quite forget--Oh, the garish years," she wailed, "since then! And how I hated you, William--and yet liked you, too,--because you were never the boy that I remembered, and people would not let you be! And how I hated them--the huzzies! For I had to see you almost every day, and it was never you I saw--Ah, William, come back for just a little, little while, and be an honest boy for just the moment that we are dying, and not an elegant fine gentleman!"

"Nay, my dear," the dramatist composedly answered, "an hour of naked candor is at hand. Life is a masquerade where Death, it would appear, is master of the ceremonies. Now he sounds his whistle; and we who went about the world so long as harlequins must unmask, and for all time put aside our abhorrence of the disheveled. For in sober verity, this is Death who comes, Olivia,--though I had thought that at his advent one would be afraid."

Yet apprehension of this gross and unavoidable adventure, so soon to be endured, thrilled him, and none too lightly. It seemed unfair that death should draw near thus sensibly, with never a twinge or ache to herald its arrival. Why, there were fifty years of life in this fine, nimble body but for any contretemps like that of the deplorable present! Thus his meditations stumbled.

"Oh, William," Lady Drogheda bewailed, "it is all so big--the incurious west, and the sea, and these rocks that were old in Noah's youth,--and we are so little----!"

"Yes," he returned, and took her hand, because their feet were wetted now; "the trap and its small prey are not commensurate. The stage is set for a Homeric death-scene, and we two profane an over-ambitious background. For who are we that Heaven should have rived the world before time was, to trap us, and should make of the old sea a fowling-net?" Their eyes encountered, and he said, with a strange gush of manliness: "Yet Heaven is kind. I am bound even in honor now to marry Mistress Araminta; and you would marry Remon in the end, Olivia,--ah, yes! for we are merely moths, my dear, and luxury is a disastrously brilliant lamp. But here are only you and I and the master of all ceremony. And yet--I would we were a little worthier, Olivia!"

"You have written four merry comedies and you were the first gentleman in England to wear a neckcloth of Flanders lace," she answered, and her smile was sadder than weeping.

"And you were the first person of quality to eat cheese-cakes in Spring Garden. There you have our epitaphs, if we in truth have earned an epitaph who have not ever lived."

"No, we have only laughed--Laugh now, for the last time, and hearten me, my handsome William! And yet could I but come to God," the woman said, with a new voice, "and make it clear to Him just how it all fell out, and beg for one more chance! How heartily I would pray then!"

"And I would cry Amen to all that prayer must of necessity contain," he answered. "Oh!" said Wycherley, "just for applause and bodily comfort and the envy of innumerable other fools we two have bartered a great heritage! I think our corner of the world will lament us for as much as a week; but I fear lest Heaven may not condescend to set apart the needful time wherein to frame a suitable chastisement for such poor imbeciles. Olivia, I have loved you all my life, and I have been faithful neither to you nor to myself! I love you so that I am not afraid even now, since you are here, and so entirely that I have forgotten how to plead my cause convincingly. And I have had practice, let me tell you. . . . !" Then he shook his head and smiled. "But candor is not *a la mode*. See, now, to what outmoded and bucolic frenzies nature brings even us at last."

She answered only, as she motioned seaward, "Look!"

And what Mr. Wycherley saw was a substantial boat rowed by four of Mr. Minifie's attendants; and in the bow of the vessel sat that wounded gentleman himself, regarding Wycherley and Lady Drogheda with some disfavor; and beside the younger man was Mistress Araminta Vining.

It was a perturbed Minifie who broke the silence. "This is very awkward," he said, "because Araminta and I are eloping. We mean to be married this same night at Milanor. And deuce take it, Mr. Wycherley! I can't leave you there to drown, any more than in the circumstances I can ask you to make one of the party."

"Mr. Wycherley," said his companion, with far more asperity, "the vanity and obduracy of a cruel father have forced me to the adoption of this desperate measure. Toward yourself I entertain no ill-feeling, nor indeed any sentiment at all except the most profound contempt. My aunt will, of course, accompany us; for yourself, you will do as you please; but in any event I solemnly protest that I spurn your odious pretensions, release myself hereby from an enforced and hideous obligation, and in a phrase would not marry you in order to be Queen of England."

"Miss Vining, I had hitherto admired you," the beau replied, with fervor, "but now esteem is changed to adoration."

Then he turned to his Olivia. "Madam, you will pardon the awkward but unavoidable publicity of my proceeding. I am a ruined man. I owe your brother-in-law some L1500, and, oddly enough, I mean to pay him. I must sell Jephcot and Skene Minor, but while life lasts I shall keep Bessington and all its memories. Meanwhile there is a clergyman waiting at Milanor. So marry me to-night, Olivia; and we will go back to Bessington to-morrow."

"To Bessington----!" she said. It was as though she spoke of something very sacred. Then very musically Lady Drogheda laughed, and to the eye she was all flippancy. "La, William, I can't bury myself in the country until the end of time," she said, "and make interminable custards," she added, "and superintend the poultry," she said, "and for recreation play short whist with the vicar."

And it seemed to Mr. Wycherley that he had gone divinely mad. "Don't lie to me, Olivia. You are thinking there are yet a host of heiresses who would be glad to be a famous beau's wife at however dear a cost. But don't lie to me. Don't even try to seem the airy and bedizened woman I have known so long. All that is over now. Death tapped us on the shoulder, and, if only for a moment, the masks were dropped.   And life is changed now, oh, everything is changed!   Then, come, my dear! let us be wise and very honest.   Let us concede it is still possible for me to find another heiress, and for you to marry Remon; let us grant it the only outcome of our common-sense! and for all that, laugh, and fling away the pottage, and be more wise than reason."

She irresolutely said: "I cannot.   Matters are altered now.   It would be madness----"

"It would undoubtedly be madness," Mr. Wycherley assented.   "But then I am so tired of being rational!   Oh, Olivia," this former arbiter of taste absurdly babbled, "if I lose you now it is forever! and there is no health in me save when I am with you.   Then alone I wish to do praiseworthy things, to be all which the boy we know of should have grown to. . . .   See how profoundly shameless I am become when, with such an audience, I take refuge in the pitiful base argument of my own weakness!   But, my dear, I want you so that nothing else in the world means anything to me.   I want you! and all my life I have wanted you."

"Boy, boy----!" she answered, and her fine hands had come to Wycherley, as white birds flutter homeward.   But even then she had to deliberate the matter--since the habits of many years are not put aside like outworn gloves,--and for innumerable centuries, it seemed to him, her foot tapped on that wetted ledge.

Presently her lashes lifted.   "I suppose it would be lacking in reverence to keep a clergyman waiting longer than was absolutely necessary?" she hazarded.

A BROWN WOMAN

A critical age called for symmetry, and exquisite finish had to be studied as much as nobility of thought. . . . POPE aimed to take first place as a writer of polished verse. Any knowledge he gained of the world, or any suggestion that came to him from his intercourse with society, was utilized to accomplish his main purpose. To put his thoughts into choice language was not enough. Each idea had to be put in its neatest and most epigrammatic form."

Why did I write? what sin to me unknown
Dipt me in ink, my parents', or my own?
As yet a child, nor yet a fool to fame,
I lisped in numbers, for the numbers came.
The muse but served to ease some friend, not wife,
To help me through this long disease, my life.

*   *   *   *   *   *

Who shames a scribbler? break one cobweb through,
He spins the slight, self-pleasing thread anew;
Destroy his fib or sophistry in vain,
The creature's at his foolish work again,
Throned in the centre of his thin designs,
Proud of a vast extent of flimsy lines!

ALEXANDER POPE.--Epistle to Dr. Arbuthnot.

A BROWN WOMAN

"But I must be hurrying home now," the girl said, "for it is high time I were back in the hayfields."

"Fair shepherdess," he implored, "for heaven's sake, let us not cut short the *pastorelle* thus abruptly."

"And what manner of beast may that be, pray?"

"'Tis a conventional form of verse, my dear, which we at present strikingly illustrate. The plan of a *pastorelle* is simplicity's self: a gentleman, which I may fairly claim to be, in some fair rural scene--such as this--comes suddenly upon a rustic maiden of surpassing beauty. He naturally falls in love with her, and they say all manner of fine things to each other."

She considered him for a while before speaking. It thrilled him to see the odd tenderness that was in her face. "You always think of saying and writing fine things, do you not, sir?"

"My dear," he answered, gravely, "I believe that I was undoubtedly guilty of such folly until you came. I wish I could make you understand how your coming has changed everything."

"You can tell me some other time," the girl gaily declared, and was about to leave him.

His hand detained her very gently. "Faith, but I fear not, for already my old hallucinations seem to me incredible. Why, yesterday I thought it the most desirable of human lots to be a great poet"--the gentleman laughed in self-mockery. "I positively did. I labored every day toward becoming one. I lived among books, esteemed that I was doing something of genuine importance as I gravely tinkered with alliteration and metaphor and antithesis and judicious paraphrases of the ancients. I put up with life solely because it afforded material for versification; and, in reality, believed the destruction of Troy was providentially ordained lest Homer lack subject matter for an epic. And as for loving, I thought people fell in love in order to exchange witty rhymes."

His hand detained her, very gently. . . . Indeed, it seemed to him he could never tire of noting her excellencies. Perhaps it was that splendid light poise of her head he chiefly loved; he thought so at least, just now. Or was it the wonder of her walk, which made all other women he had ever known appear to mince and hobble, like rusty toys? Something there was assuredly about this slim brown girl which recalled an untamed and harmless woodland creature; and it was that, he knew, which most poignantly moved him, even though he could not name it. Perhaps it was her bright kind eyes, which seemed to mirror the tranquillity of forests. . . .

"You gentry are always talking of love," she marveled.

"Oh," he said, with acerbity, "oh, I don't doubt that any number of beef-gorging squires and leering, long-legged Oxford dandies----" He broke off here, and laughed contemptuously. "Well, you are beautiful, and they have eyes as keen as mine. And I do not blame you, my dear, for believing my designs to be no more commendable than theirs--no, not at all."

But his mood was spoiled, and his tetchy vanity hurt, by the thought of stout well-set fellows having wooed this girl; and he permitted her to go without protest.

Yet he sat alone for a while upon the fallen tree-trunk, humming a contented little tune. Never in his life had he been happier. He did not venture to suppose that any creature so adorable could love such a sickly hunchback, such a gargoyle of a man, as he was; but that Sarah was fond of him, he knew. There would be no trouble in arranging with her father for their marriage, most certainly; and he meant to attend to that matter this very morning, and within ten minutes. So Mr. Alexander Pope was meanwhile arranging in his mind a suitable wording for his declaration of marital aspirations.

Thus John Gay found him presently and roused him from phrase-spinning. "And what shall we do this morning, Alexander?" Gay was always demanding, like a spoiled child, to be amused.

Pope told him what his own plans were, speaking quite simply, but with his countenance radiant. Gay took off his hat and wiped his forehead, for the day was warm. He did not say anything at all.

"Well----?" Mr. Pope asked, after a pause.

Mr. Gay was dubious. "I had never thought that you would marry," he said. "And--why, hang it, Alexander! to grow enamored of a milkmaid is well enough for the hero of a poem, but in a poet it hints at injudicious composition."

Mr. Pope gesticulated with thin hands and seemed upon the verge of eloquence. Then he spoke unanswerably. "But I love her," he said.

John Gay's reply was a subdued whistle. He, in common with the other guests of Lord Harcourt, at Nuneham Courtney, had wondered what would be the outcome of Mr. Alexander Pope's intimacy with Sarah Drew. A month earlier the poet had sprained his ankle upon Amshot Heath, and this young woman had found him lying there, entirely helpless, as she returned from her evening milking. Being hale of person, she had managed to get the little hunchback to her home unaided. And since then Pope had often been seen with her.

This much was common knowledge. That Mr. Pope proposed to marry the heroine of his misadventure afforded a fair mark for raillery, no doubt, but Gay, in common with the run of educated England in 1718, did not aspire to be facetious at Pope's expense. The luxury was too costly. Offend the dwarf in any fashion, and were you the proudest duke at Court or the most inconsiderable rhymester in Petticoat Lane, it made no difference; there was no crime too heinous for "the great Mr. Pope's" next verses to charge you with, and, worst of all, there was no misdoing so out of character that his adroit malignancy could not make it seem plausible.

Now, after another pause, Pope said, "I must be going now. Will you not wish me luck?"

"Why, Alexander--why, hang it!" was Mr. Gay's observation, "I believe that you are human after all, and not just a book in breeches."

He thereby voiced a commentary patently uncalled-for, as Mr. Pope afterward reflected. Mr. Pope was then treading toward the home of old Frederick Drew. It was a gray morning in late July.

"I love her," Pope had said. The fact was undeniable; yet an expression of it necessarily halts. Pope knew, as every man must do who dares conserve his energies to annotate the drama of life rather than play a part in it, the nature of that loneliness which this conservation breeds. Such persons may hope to win a posthumous esteem in the library, but it is at the bleak cost of making life a wistful transaction with foreigners. In such enforced aloofness Sarah Drew had come to him--strong, beautiful, young, good and vital, all that he was not--and had serenely befriended "the great Mr. Pope," whom she viewed as a queer decrepit little gentleman of whom within a week she was unfeignedly fond.

"I love her," Pope had said. Eh, yes, no doubt; and what, he fiercely demanded of himself, was he--a crippled scribbler, a bungling artisan of phrases--that he should dare to love this splendid and deep-bosomed goddess? Something of youth awoke, possessing him--something of that high ardor which, as he cloudily remembered now, had once controlled a boy who dreamed in Windsor Forest and with the lightest of hearts planned to achieve the impossible. For what is more difficult of attainment than to achieve the perfected phrase, so worded that to alter a syllable of its wording would be little short of sacrilege?

"What whimwhams!" decreed the great Mr. Pope, aloud. "Verse-making is at best only the affair of idle men who write in their closets and of idle men who read there. And as for him who polishes phrases, whatever be his fate in poetry, it is ten to one but he must give up all the reasonable aims of life for it."

No, he would have no more of loneliness. Henceforward Alexander Pope would be human--like the others. To write perfectly was much; but it was not everything. Living was capable of furnishing even more than the raw material of a couplet. It might, for instance, yield content.

For instance, if you loved, and married, and begot, and died, with the seriousness of a person who believes he is performing an action of real importance, and conceded that the perfection of any art, whether it be that of verse-making or of rope-dancing, is at best a by-product of life's conduct; at worst, you probably would not be lonely. No; you would be at one with all other fat-witted people, and there was no greater blessing conceivable.

Pope muttered, and produced his notebook, and wrote tentatively.

Wrote Mr. Pope:

The bliss of man (could pride that blessing find)
Is not to act or think beyond mankind;
No powers of body or of soul to share
But what his nature and his state can bear.

"His state!" yes, undeniably, two sibilants collided here. "His wit?"--no, that would be flat-footed awkwardness in the management of your vowel-sounds; the lengthened "a" was almost requisite. . . . Pope was fretting over the imbroglio when he absent-mindedly glanced up to perceive that his Sarah, not irrevocably offended, was being embraced by a certain John Hughes--who was a stalwart, florid personable individual, no doubt, but, after all, only an unlettered farmer.

The dwarf gave a hard, wringing motion of his hands. The diamond-Lord Bolingbroke's gift--which ornamented Pope's left hand cut into the flesh of his little finger, so cruel was the gesture; and this little finger was bleeding as Pope tripped forward, smiling. A gentleman does not incommode the public by obtruding the ugliness of a personal wound.

"Do I intrude?" he queried. "Ah, well! I also have dwelt in Arcadia." It was bitter to comprehend that he had never done so.

The lovers were visibly annoyed; yet, if an interruption of their pleasant commerce was decreed to be, it could not possibly have sprung, as they soon found, from a more sympathetic source.

These were not subtle persons. Pope had the truth from them within ten minutes. They loved each other; but John Hughes was penniless, and old Frederick Drew was, in consequence, obdurate.

"And, besides, he thinks you mean to marry her!" said John Hughes.

"My dear man, he pardonably forgets that the utmost reach of my designs in common reason would be to have her as my kept mistress for a month or two," drawled Mr. Pope. "As concerns yourself, my good fellow, the case is somewhat different. Why, it is a veritable romance--an affair of Daphne and Corydon--although, to be unpardonably candid, the plot of your romance, my young Arcadians, is not the most original conceivable. I think that the denouement need not baffle our imaginations."

The dwarf went toward Sarah Drew. The chary sunlight had found the gold in her hair, and its glint was brightly visible to him. "My dear--" he said. His thin long fingers touched her capable hand. It was a sort of caress--half-timid. "My dear, I owe my life to you. My body is at most a flimsy abortion such as a night's exposure would have made more tranquil than it is just now. Yes, it was you who found a caricature of the sort of man that Mr. Hughes here is, disabled, helpless, and--for reasons which doubtless seemed to you sufficient--contrived that this unsightly parody continue in existence. I am not lovable, my dear. I am only a hunchback, as you can see. My aspirations and my sickly imaginings merit only the derision of a candid clean-souled being such as you are." His finger-tips touched the back of her hand again. "I think there was never a maker of enduring verse who did not at one period or another long to exchange an assured immortality for a sturdier pair of shoulders. I think--I think that I am prone to speak at random," Pope said, with his half-drowsy smile. "Yet, none the less, an honest man, as our kinsmen in Adam average, is bound to pay his equitable debts."

She said, "I do not understand."

"I have perpetrated certain jingles," Pope returned. "I had not comprehended until to-day they are the only children I shall leave behind me. Eh, and what would you make of them, my dear, could ingenuity contrive a torture dire enough to force you into reading them! . . . Misguided people have paid me for contriving these jingles. So that I have money enough to buy you from your father just as I would purchase one of his heifers. Yes, at the very least I have money, and I have earned it. I will send your big-thewed adorer--I believe that Hughes is the name?--L500 of it this afternoon. That sum, I gather, will be sufficient to remove your father's objection to your marriage with Mr. Hughes."

Pope could not but admire himself tremendously. Moreover, in such matters no woman is blind. Tears came into Sarah's huge brown eyes. This tenderhearted girl was not thinking of John Hughes now. Pope noted the fact with the pettiest exultation. "Oh, you--you are good." Sarah Drew spoke as with difficulty.

"No adjective, my dear, was ever applied with less discrimination. It is merely that you have rendered no inconsiderable service to posterity, and merit a reward."

"Oh, and indeed, indeed, I was always fond of you----" The girl sobbed this.

She would have added more, no doubt, since compassion is garrulous, had not Pope's scratched hand dismissed a display of emotion as not entirely in consonance with the rules of the game.

"My dear, therein you have signally honored me. There remains only to offer you my appreciation of your benevolence toward a sickly monster, and to entreat for my late intrusion--however unintentional--that forgiveness which you would not deny, I think, to any other impertinent insect."

"Oh, but we have no words to thank you, sir----!" Thus Hughes began.

"Then don't attempt it, my good fellow. For phrase-spinning, as I can assure you, is the most profitless of all pursuits." Whereupon Pope bowed low, wheeled, walked away. Yes, he was wounded past sufferance; it seemed to him he must die of it. Life was a farce, and Destiny an overseer who hiccoughed mandates. Well, all that even Destiny could find to gloat over, he reflected, was the tranquil figure of a smallish gentleman switching at the grass-blades with his cane as he sauntered under darkening skies.

For a storm was coming on, and the first big drops of it were splattering the terrace when Mr. Pope entered Lord Harcourt's mansion.

Pope went straight to his own rooms. As he came in there was a vivid flash of lightning, followed instantaneously by a crashing, splitting noise, like that of universes ripped asunder. He did not honor the high uproar with attention. This dwarf was not afraid of anything except the commission of an error in taste.

Then, too, there were letters for him, laid ready on the writing-table. Nothing of much importance he found there.--Here, though, was a rather diverting letter from Eustace Budgell, that poor fool, abjectly thanking Mr. Pope for his advice concerning how best to answer the atrocious calumnies on Budgell then appearing in *The Grub-Street Journal*,--and reposing, drolly enough, next the proof-sheets of an anonymous letter Pope had prepared for the forthcoming issue of that publication, wherein he sprightlily told how Budgell had poisoned Dr. Tindal, after forging his will. For even if Budgell had not in point of fact been guilty of these particular peccadilloes, he had quite certainly committed the crime of speaking lightly of Mr. Pope, as "a little envious animal," some seven years ago; and it was for this grave indiscretion that Pope was dexterously goading the man into insanity, and eventually drove him to suicide. . . .

The storm made the room dark and reading difficult. Still, this was an even more amusing letter, from the all-powerful Duchess of Marlborough. In as civil terms as her sick rage could muster, the frightened woman offered Mr. Pope L1,000 to suppress his verbal portrait of her, in the character of Atossa, from his *Moral Essays*; and Pope straightway decided to accept the bribe, and afterward to print his verses unchanged. For the hag, as he reflected, very greatly needed to be taught that in this world there was at least one person who did not quail before her tantrums. There would be, moreover, even an elementary justice in thus robbing her who had robbed England at large. And, besides, her name was Sarah. . . .

Pope lighted four candles and set them before the long French mirror. He stood appraising his many curious deformities while the storm raged. He stood sidelong, peering over his left shoulder, in order to see the outline of his crooked back. Nowhere in England, he reflected, was there a person more pitiable and more repellent outwardly.

"And, oh, it would be droll," Pope said, aloud, "if our exteriors were ever altogether parodies. But time keeps a diary in our faces, and writes a monstrously plain hand. Now, if you take the first letter of Mr. Alexander Pope's Christian name, and the first and last letters of his surname, you have A. P. E.," Pope quoted, genially. "I begin to think that Dennis was right. What conceivable woman would not prefer a well-set man of five-and-twenty to such a withered abortion? And what does it matter, after all, that a hunchback has dared to desire a shapely brown-haired woman?"

Pope came more near to the mirror. "Make answer, you who have dared to imagine that a goddess was ever drawn to descend into womanhood except by kisses, brawn and a clean heart."

Another peal of thunder bellowed. The storm was growing furious. "Yet I have had a marvelous dream. Now I awaken. I must go on in the old round. As long as my wits preserve their agility I must be able to amuse, to flatter and, at need, to intimidate the patrons of that ape in the mirror, so that they will not dare refuse me the market-value of my antics. And Sarah Drew has declined an alliance such as this in favor of a fresh-colored complexion and a pair of straight shoulders!"

Pope thought a while. "And a clean heart! She bargained royally, giving love for nothing less than love. The man is rustic, illiterate; he never heard of Aristotle, he would be at a loss to distinguish between a trochee and a Titian, and if you mentioned Boileau to him would probably imagine you were talking of cookery. But he loves her. He would forfeit eternity to save her a toothache. And, chief of all, she can make this robust baby happy, and she alone can make him happy. And so, she gives, gives royally--she gives, God bless her!"

Rain, sullen rain, was battering the window. "And you--you hunchback in the mirror, you maker of neat rhymes--pray, what had you to offer? A coach-and-six, of course, and pin-money and furbelows and in the end a mausoleum with unimpeachable Latin on it! And--pate sur pate--an unswerving devotion which she would share on almost equal terms with the Collected Works of Alexander Pope. And so she chose--chose brawn and a clean heart."

The dwarf turned, staggered, fell upon his bed. "God, make a man of me, make me a good brave man. I loved her--oh, such as I am, You know that I loved her! You know that I desire her happiness above all things. Ah, no, for You know that I do not at bottom. I want to hurt, to wound all living creatures, because they know how to be happy, and I do not know how. Ah, God, and why did You decree that I should never be an obtuse and comely animal such as this John Hughes is? I am so tired of being 'the great Mr. Pope,' and I want only the common joys of life."

The hunchback wept. It would be too curious to anatomize the writhings of his proud little spirit.

Now some one tapped upon the door. It was John Gay. He was bidden to enter, and, complying, found Mr. Pope yawning over the latest of Tonson's publications.

Gay's face was singularly portentous. "My friend," Gay blurted out, "I bring news which will horrify you. Believe me, I would never have mustered the pluck to bring it did I not love you. I cannot let you hear it first in public and unprepared, as, otherwise, you would have to do."

"Do I not know you have the kindest heart in all the world? Why, so outrageous are your amiable defects that they would be the public derision of your enemies if you had any," Pope returned.

The other poet evinced an awkward comminglement of consternation and pity. "It appears that when this storm arose--why, Mistress Drew was with a young man of the neighborhood--a John Hewet----" Gay was speaking with unaccustomed rapidity.

"Hughes, I think," Pope interrupted, equably.

"Perhaps--I am not sure. They sought shelter under a haycock. You will remember that first crash of thunder, as if the heavens were in demolishment? My friend, the reapers who had been laboring in the fields--who had been driven to such protection as the trees or hedges afforded----"

"Get on!" a shrill voice cried; "for God's love, man, get on!" Mr. Pope had risen. This pallid shaken wisp was not in appearance the great Mr. Pope whose ingenuity had enabled Homeric warriors to excel in the genteel.

"They first saw a little smoke. . . . They found this Hughes with one arm about the neck of Mistress Drew, and the other held over her face, as if to screen her from the lightning. They were both"--and here Gay hesitated. "They were both dead," he amended.

Pope turned abruptly. Nakedness is of necessity uncouth, he held, whether it be the body or the soul that is unveiled. Mr. Pope went toward a window which he opened, and he stood thus looking out for a brief while.

"So she is dead," he said. "It is very strange. So many rare felicities of curve and color, so much of purity and kindliness and valor and mirth, extinguished as one snuffs a candle! Well! I am sorry she is dead, for the child had a talent for living and got such joy out of it. . . . Hers was a lovely happy life, but it was sterile. Already nothing remains of her but dead flesh which must be huddled out of sight. I shall not perish thus entirely, I believe. Men will remember me. Truly a mighty foundation for pride! when the utmost I can hope for is but to be read in one island, and to be thrown aside at the end of one age. Indeed, I am not even sure of that much. I print, and print, and print. And when I collect my verses into books, I am altogether uncertain whether to took upon myself as a man building a monument, or burying the dead. It sometimes seems to me that each publication is but a solemn funeral of many wasted years. For I have given all to the verse-making. Granted that the sacrifice avails to rescue my name from oblivion, what will it profit me when I am dead and care no more for men's opinions than Sarah Drew cares now for what I say of her? But then she never cared. She loved John Hughes. And she was right."

He made an end of speaking, still peering out of the window with considerate narrowed eyes.

The storm was over. In the beech-tree opposite a wren was raising optimistic outcry. The sun had won his way through a black-bellied shred of cloud; upon the terrace below, a dripping Venus and a Perseus were glistening as with white fire. Past these, drenched gardens, the natural wildness of which was judiciously restrained with walks, ponds, grottoes, statuary and other rural elegancies, displayed the intermingled brilliancies of diamonds and emeralds, and glittered as with pearls and rubies where tempest-battered roses were reviving in assertiveness.

"I think the storm is over," Mr. Pope remarked. "It is strange how violent are these convulsions of nature. . . . But nature is a treacherous blowsy jade, who respects nobody. A gentleman can but shrug under her onslaughts, and hencefor-ward civilly avoid them. It is a consolation to reflect that they pass quickly."

He turned as in defiance. "Yes, yes! It hurts. But I envy them. Yes, even I, that ugly spiteful hornet of a man! 'the great Mr. Pope,' who will be dining with the proudest people in England within the hour and gloating over their deference! For they presume to make a little free with God occasionally, John, but never with me. And *I* envy these dead young fools. . . . You see, they loved each other, John. I left them, not an hour ago, the happiest of living creatures. I looked back once. I pretended to have dropped my handkerchief. I imagine they were talking of their wedding-clothes, for this broad-shouldered Hughes was matching poppies and field-flowers to her complexion. It was a scene out of Theocritus. I think Heaven was so well pleased by the tableau that Heaven hastily resumed possession of its enactors in order to prevent any after-happenings from belittling that perfect instant."

"Egad, and matrimony might easily have proved an anti-climax," Gay consid-ered.

"Yes; oh, it is only Love that is blind, and not the lover necessarily. I know. I suppose I always knew at the bottom of my heart. This hamadryad was destined in the outcome to dwindle into a village housewife, she would have taken a lively in-terest in the number of eggs the hens were laying, she would even have assured her children, precisely in the way her father spoke of John Hughes, that young people ordinarily have foolish fancies which their rational elders agree to disregard. But as it is, no Eastern queen--not Semele herself--left earth more nobly--"

Pope broke off short. He produced his notebook, which he never went with-out, and wrote frowningly, with many erasures. "H'm, yes," he said; and he read aloud:

"When Eastern lovers feed the funeral fire,   On the same pile the faithful fair expire; Here pitying heaven that virtue mutual found,   And blasted both that it might neither wound.   Hearts so sincere the Almighty saw well pleased, Sent His own lightning and the victims seized."

Then Pope made a grimace. "No; the analogy is trim enough, but the lines lack fervor. It is deplorable how much easier it is to express any emotion other than that of which one is actually conscious." Pope had torn the paper half-through before he reflected that it would help to fill a printed page. He put it in his pocket. "But, come now, I am writing to Lady Mary this afternoon. You know how she loves oddities. Between us--with prose as the medium, of course, since verse should, after all, confine itself to the commemoration of heroes and royal persons--I believe we might make of this occurrence a neat and moving *pastorelle*--I should say, pastoral, of course, but my wits are wool-gathering."

Mr. Gay had the kindest heart in the universe. Yet he, also, had dreamed of the perfected phrase, so worded that to alter a syllable of its wording would be little short of sacrilege. Eyes kindling, he took up a pen. "Yes, yes, I understand. Egad, it is an admirable subject. But, then, I don't believe I ever saw these lovers----?"

"John was a well-set man of about five-and-twenty," replied Mr. Pope; "and Sarah was a brown woman of eighteen years, three months and fourteen days."

Then these two dipped their pens and set about a moving composition, which has to-day its proper rating among Mr. Pope's Complete Works.

PRO HONORIA

But that sense of negation, of theoretic insecurity, which was in the air, conspiring with what was of like tendency in himself, made of Lord UF-FORD a central type of disillusion. . . . He had been amiable because the general betise of humanity did not in his opinion greatly matter, after all; and in reading these 'SATIRES' it is well-nigh painful to witness the blind and naked forces of nature and circumstance surprising him in the uncontrollable movements of his own so carefully guarded heart."

> Why is a handsome wife adored
> By every coxcomb but her lord?
>
> From yonder puppet-man inquire
> Who wisely hides his wood and wire;
> Shows Sheba's queen completely dress'd
> And Solomon in royal vest;
>
> But view them litter'd on the floor,
> Or strung on pegs behind the door,
> Punch is exactly of a piece
> With Lorrain's duke, and prince of Greece.

HORACE CALVERLEY.--Petition to the Duke of Ormskirk.

PRO HONORIA

In the early winter of 1761 the Earl of Bute, then Secretary of State, gave vent to an outburst of unaccustomed profanity. Mr. Robert Calverley, who represented England at the Court of St. Petersburg, had resigned his office without prelude or any word of explanation. This infuriated Bute, since his pet scheme was to make peace with Russia and thereby end the Continental War. Now all was to do again; the minister raged, shrugged, furnished a new emissary with credentials, and marked Calverley's name for punishment.

As much, indeed, was written to Calverley by Lord Ufford, the poet, diarist, musician and virtuoso:

Our Scottish Mortimer, it appears, is unwilling to have the map of Europe altered because Mr. Robert Calverley has taken a whim to go into Italy. He is angrier than I have ever known him to be. He swears that with a pen's flourish you have imperiled the well-being of England, and raves in the same breath of the preferment he had designed for you. Beware of him. For my own part, I shrug and acquiesce, because I am familiar with your pranks. I merely venture to counsel that you do not crown the Pelion of abuse, which our statesmen are heaping upon you, with the Ossa of physical as well as political suicide. Hasten on your Italian jaunt, for Umfraville, who is now with me at Carberry Hill, has publicly declared that if you dare re-appear in England he will have you horsewhipped by his footmen. In consequence, I would most earnestly advise----

Mr. Calverley read no further, but came straightway into England. He had not been in England since his elopement, three years before that spring, with the Marquis of Umfraville's betrothed, Lord Radnor's daughter, whom Calverley had married at Calais. Mr. Calverley and his wife were presently at Carberry Hill, Lord Ufford's home, where, arriving about moon-rise, they found a ball in progress.

Their advent caused a momentary check to merriment. The fiddlers ceased, because Lord Ufford had signaled them. The fine guests paused in their stately dance. Lord Ufford, in a richly figured suit, came hastily to Lady Honoria Calverley, his high heels tapping audibly upon the floor, and with gallantry lifted her hand toward his lips. Her husband he embraced, and the two men kissed each other, as was the custom of the age. Chatter and laughter rose on every side as pert and merry as the noises of a brook in springtime.

"I fear that as Lord Umfraville's host," young Calverley at once began, "you cannot with decorum convey to the ignoramus my opinion as to his ability to conjugate the verb **to dare**."

"Why, but no! you naturally demand a duel," the poet-earl returned. "It is very like you. I lament your decision, but I will attempt to arrange the meeting for tomorrow morning."

Lord Ufford smiled and nodded to the musicians. He finished the dance to admiration, as this lean dandified young man did everything--"assiduous to win each fool's applause," as his own verses scornfully phrase it. Then Ufford went about his errand of death and conversed for a long while with Umfraville.

Afterward Lord Ufford beckoned to Calverley, who shrugged and returned Mr. Erwyn's snuff-box, which Calverley had been admiring. He followed the earl into a side-room opening upon the Venetian Chamber wherein the fete was. Ufford closed the door. You saw that he had put away the exterior of mirth that hospitality demanded of him, and perturbation showed in the lean countenance which was by ordinary so proud and so amiably peevish.

"Robin, you have performed many mad actions in your life!" he said; "but this return into the three kingdoms out-Herods all! Did I not warn you against Umfraville!"

"Why, certainly you did," returned Mr. Calverley. "You informed me--which was your duty as a friend--of this curmudgeon's boast that he would have me horsewhipped if I dared venture into England. You will readily conceive that any gentleman of self-respect cannot permit such farcical utterances to be delivered without appending a gladiatorial epilogue. Well! what are the conditions of this duel?"

"Oh, fool that I have been!" cried Ufford, who was enabled now by virtue of their seclusion to manifest his emotion. "I, who have known you all your life----!"

He paced the room. Pleading music tinged the silence almost insensibly.

"Heh, Fate has an imperial taste in humor!" the poet said. "Robin, we have been more than brothers. And it is I, I, of all persons living, who have drawn you into this imbroglio!"

"My danger is not very apparent as yet," said Calverley, "if Umfraville controls his sword no better than his tongue."

My lord of Ufford went on: "There is no question of a duel. It is as well to spare you what Lord Umfraville replied to my challenge. Let it suffice that we do not get sugar from the snake. Besides, the man has his grievance. Robin, have you forgot that necklace you and Pevensey took from Umfraville some three years ago--before you went into Russia?"

Calverley laughed. The question recalled an old hot-headed time when, exalted to a frolicsome zone by the discovery of Lady Honoria Pomfret's love for him, he planned the famous jest which he and the mad Earl of Pevensey perpetrated upon Umfraville. This masquerade won quick applause. Persons of ton guffawed like ploughboys over the discomfiture of an old hunks thus divertingly stripped of his bride, all his betrothal gifts, and of the very clothes he wore. An anonymous scribbler had detected in the occurrence a denouement suited to the stage and had constructed a comedy around it, which, when produced by the Duke's company, had won acclaim from hilarious auditors.

So Calverley laughed heartily. "Gad, what a jest that was! This Umfraville comes to marry Honoria. And highwaymen attack his coach! I would give L50 to have witnessed this usurer's arrival at Denton Honor in his underclothes! and to have seen his monkey-like grimaces when he learned that Honoria and I were already across the Channel!"

"You robbed him, though----"

"Indeed, for beginners at peculation we did not do so badly. We robbed him and his valet of everything in the coach, including their breeches. You do not mean that Pevensey has detained the poor man's wedding trousers? If so, it is unfortunate, because this loud-mouthed miser has need of them in order that he may be handsomely interred."

"Lord Umfraville's wedding-suit was stuffed with straw, hung on a pole and paraded through London by Pevensey, March, Selwyn and some dozen other madcaps, while six musicians marched before them. The clothes were thus conveyed to Umfraville's house. I think none of us would have relished a joke like that were he the butt of it."

Now the poet's lean countenance was turned upon young Calverley, and as always, Ufford evoked that nobility in Calverley which follies veiled but had not ever killed.

"Egad," said Robert Calverley; "I grant you that all this was infamously done. I never authorized it. I shall kill Pevensey. Indeed, I will do more," he added, with a flourish. "For I will apologize to Umfraville, and this very night."

But Ufford was not disposed to levity. "Let us come to the point," he sadly said. "Pevensey returned everything except the necklace which Umfraville had intended to be his bridal gift. Pevensey conceded the jest, in fine; and denied all knowledge of any necklace."

It was an age of accommodating morality. Calverley sketched a whistle, and showed no other trace of astonishment.

"I see. The fool confided in the spendthrift. My dear, I understand. In nature Pevensey gave the gems to some nymph of Sadler's Wells or Covent Garden. For I was out of England. And so he capped his knavery with insolence. It is an additional reason why Pevensey should not live to scratch a gray head. It is, however, an affront to me that Umfraville should have believed him. I doubt if I may overlook that, Horace?"

"I question if he did believe. But, then, what help had he? This Pevensey is an earl. His person as a peer of England is inviolable. No statute touches him directly, because he may not be confined except by the King's personal order. And it is tolerably notorious that Pevensey is in Lord Bute's pay, and that our Scottish Mortimer, to do him justice, does not permit his spies to be injured."

Now Mr. Calverley took snuff. The music without was now more audible, and it had shifted to a merrier tune.

"I think I comprehend. Pevensey and I--whatever were our motives--have committed a robbery. Pevensey, as the law runs, is safe. I, too, was safe as long as I kept out of England. As matters stand, Lord Umfraville intends to press a charge of theft against me. And I am in disgrace with Bute, who is quite content to beat offenders with a crooked stick. This confluence of two-penny accidents is annoying."

"It is worse than you know," my lord of Ufford returned. He opened the door which led to the Venetian Chamber. A surge of music, of laughter, and of many lights invaded the room wherein they stood. "D'ye see those persons, just past Umfraville, so inadequately disguised as gentlemen? They are from Bow Street. Lord Umfraville intends to apprehend you here to-night."

"He has an eye for the picturesque," drawled Calverley. "My tragedy, to do him justice, could not be staged more strikingly. Those additional alcoves have improved the room beyond belief. I must apologize for not having rendered my compliments a trifle earlier."

Internally he outstormed Termagaunt. It was infamous enough, in all conscience, to be arrested, but to have half the world of fashion as witnessess of ones discomfiture was perfectly intolerable. He recognized the excellent chance he had of being the most prominent figure upon some scaffold before long, but that contingency did not greatly trouble Calverley, as set against the certainty of being made ridiculous within the next five minutes.

In consequence, he frowned and rearranged the fall of his shirt-frill a whit the more becomingly.

"Yes, for hate sharpens every faculty," the earl went on. "Even Umfraville understands that you do not fear death. So he means to have you tried like any common thief while all your quondam friends sit and snigger. And you will be convicted----"

"Why, necessarily, since I am not as Pevensey. Of course, I must confess I took the necklace."

"And Pevensey must stick to the tale that he knows nothing of any necklace. Dear Robin, this means Newgate. Accident deals very hardly with us, Robin, for this means Tyburn Hill."

"Yes; I suppose it means my death," young Calverley assented. "Well! I have feasted with the world and found its viands excellent. The banquet ended, I must not grumble with my host because I find his choice of cordials not altogether to my liking." Thus speaking, he was aware of nothing save that the fiddlers were now about an air to which he had often danced with his dear wife.

"I have a trick yet left to save our honor,----" Lord Ufford turned to a table where wine and glasses were set ready. "I propose a toast. Let us drink--for the last time--to the honor of the Calverleys."

"It is an invitation I may not decorously refuse. And yet--it may be that I do not understand you?"

My lord of Ufford poured wine into two glasses. These glasses were from among the curios he collected so industriously--tall, fragile things, of seventeenth century make, very intricately cut with roses and thistles, and in the bottom of each glass a three-penny piece was embedded. Lord Ufford took a tiny vial from his pocket and emptied its contents into the glass which stood the nearer to Mr. Calverley.

"This is Florence water. We dabblers in science are experimenting with it at Gresham College. A taste of it means death--a painless, quick and honorable death. You will have died of a heart seizure. Come, Robin, let us drink to the honor of the Calverleys."

The poet-earl paused for a little while. Now he was like some seer of supernal things.

"For look you," said Lord Ufford, "we come of honorable blood. We two are gentlemen. We have our code, and we may not infringe upon it. Our code does not invariably square with reason, and I doubt if Scripture would afford a dependable foundation. So be it! We have our code and we may not infringe upon it. There have been many Calverleys who did not fear their God, but there was never any one of them who did not fear dishonor. I am the head of no less proud a house. As such, I counsel you to drink and die within the moment. It is not possible a Calverley survive dishonor. Oh, God!" the poet cried, and his voice broke; "and what is honor to this clamor within me! Robin, I love you better than I do this talk of honor! For, Robin, I have loved you long! so long that what we do to-night will always make life hideous to me!"

Calverley was not unmoved, but he replied in the tone of daily intercourse. "It is undoubtedly absurd to perish here, like some unreasonable adversary of the Borgias. Your device is rather outrageously horrific, Horace, like a bit out of your own romance--yes, egad, it is pre-eminently worthy of the author of *The Vassal of Spalatro*. Still I can understand that it is preferable to having fat and greasy fellows squander a shilling for the privilege of perching upon a box while I am being hanged. And I think I shall accept your toast--

"You will be avenged," Ufford said, simply.

"My dear, as if I ever questioned that! Of course, you will kill Pevensey first and Umfraville afterward. Only I want to live. For I was meant to play a joyous role wholeheartedly in the big comedy of life. So many people find the world a dreary residence," Mr. Calverley sighed, "that it is really a pity some one of these long-faced stolidities cannot die now instead of me. For I have found life wonderful throughout."

The brows of Ufford knit. "Would you consent to live as a transported felon? I have much money. I need not tell you the last penny is at your disposal. It might be possible to bribe. Indeed, Lord Bute is all-powerful to-day and he would perhaps procure a pardon for you at my entreaty. He is so kind as to admire my scribblings. . . Or you might live among your fellow-convicts somewhere over sea for a while longer. I had not thought that such would be your choice----" Here Ufford shrugged, restrained by courtesy. "Besides, Lord Bute is greatly angered with you, because you have endangered his Russian alliance. However, if you wish it, I will try----"

"Oh, for that matter, I do not much fear Lord Bute, because I bring him the most welcome news he has had in many a day. I may tell you since it will be public to-morrow. The Tzaritza Elizabeth, our implacable enemy, died very suddenly three weeks ago. Peter of Holstein-Gottrop reigns to-day in Russia, and I have made terms with him. I came to tell Lord Bute the Cossack troops have been recalled from Prussia. The war is at an end." Young Calverley meditated and gave his customary boyish smile. "Yes, I discharged my Russian mission after all--even after I had formally relinquished it--because I was so opportunely aided by the accident of the Tzaritza's death. And Bute cares only for results. So I would explain to him that I resigned my mission simply because in Russia my wife could not have lived out another year----"

The earl exclaimed, "Then Honoria is ill!" Mr. Calverley did not attend, but stood looking out into the Venetian Chamber.

"See, Horace, she is dancing with Anchester while I wait here so near to death. She dances well. But Honoria does everything adorably. I cannot tell you--oh, not even you!--how happy these three years have been with her. Eh, well! the gods are jealous of such happiness. You will remember how her mother died? It appears that Honoria is threatened with a slow consumption, and a death such as her mother's was. She does not know. There was no need to frighten her. For although the rigors of another Russian winter, as all physicians tell me, would inevitably prove fatal to her, there is no reason why my dearest dear should not continue to laugh just as she always does--for a long, bright and happy while in some warm climate such as Italy's. In nature I resigned my appointment. I did not consider England, or my own trivial future, or anything of that sort. I considered only Honoria."

He gazed for many moments upon the woman whom he loved. His speech took on an odd simplicity.

"Oh, yes, I think that in the end Bute would procure a pardon for me. But not even Bute can override the laws of England. I would have to be tried first, and have ballads made concerning me, and be condemned, and so on. That would detain Honoria in England, because she is sufficiently misguided to love me. I could never persuade her to leave me with my life in peril. She could not possibly survive an English winter." Here Calverley evinced unbridled mirth. "The irony of events is magnificent. There is probably no question of hanging or even of transportation. It is merely certain that if I venture from this room I bring about Honoria's death as incontestably as if I strangled her with these two hands. So I choose my own death in preference. It will grieve Honoria----" His voice was not completely steady. "But she is young. She will forget me, for she forgets easily, and she will be happy. I look to you to see--even before you have killed Pevensey--that Honoria goes into Italy. For she admires and loves you, almost as much as I do, Horace, and she will readily be guided by you----"

He cried my lord of Ufford's given name some two or three times, for young Calverley had turned, and he had seen Ufford's face.

The earl moistened his lips. "You are a fool," he said, with a thin voice. "Why do you trouble me by being better than I? Or do you only posture for my benefit? Do you deal honestly with me, Robert Calverley?--then swear it----" He laughed here, very horribly. "Ah, no, when did you ever lie! You do not lie--not you!"

He waited for a while. "But I am otherwise. I dare to lie when the occasion promises. I have desired Honoria since the first moment wherein I saw her. I may tell you now. I think that you do not remember. We gathered cherries. I ate two of them which had just lain upon her knee----"

His hands had clenched each other, and his lips were drawn back so that you saw his exquisite teeth, which were ground together. He stood thus for a little, silent.

Then Ufford began again: "I planned all this. I plotted this with Umfraville. I wrote you such a letter as would inevitably draw you to your death. I wished your death. For Honoria would then be freed of you. I would condole with her. She is readily comforted, impatient of sorrow, incapable of it, I dare say. She would have married me. . . . Why must I tell you this? Oh, I am Fate's buffoon! For I have won, I have won! and there is that in me which will not accept the stake I cheated for."

"And you," said Calverley--"this thing is you!"

"A helpless reptile now," said Ufford. "I have not the power to check Lord Umfraville in his vengeance. You must be publicly disgraced, and must, I think, be hanged even now when it will not benefit me at all. It may be I shall weep for that some day! Or else Honoria must die, because an archangel could not persuade her to desert you in your peril. For she loves you--loves you to the full extent of her merry and shallow nature. Oh, I know that, as you will never know it. I shall have killed Honoria! I shall not weep when Honoria dies. Harkee, Robin! they are dancing yonder. It is odd to think that I shall never dance again."

"Horace--!" the younger man said, like a person of two minds. He seemed to choke. He gave a frantic gesture. "Oh, I have loved you. I have loved nothing as I have loved you."

"And yet you chatter of your passion for Honoria!" Lord Ufford returned, with a snarl. "I ask what proof is there of this?--Why, that you have surrendered your well-being in this world through love of her. But I gave what is vital. I was an honorable gentleman without any act in all my life for which I had need to blush. I loved you as I loved no other being in the universe." He spread his hands, which now twitched horribly. "You will never understand. It does not matter. I desired Honoria. To-day through my desire of her, I am that monstrous thing which you alone know me to be. I think I gave up much. ***Pro honoria!***" he chuckled. "The Latin halts, but, none the less, the jest is excellent."

"You have given more than I would dare to give," said Calverley. He shuddered.

"And to no end!" cried Ufford. "Ah, fate, the devil and that code I mocked are all in league to cheat me!"

Said Calverley: "The man whom I loved most is dead. Oh, had the world been searched between the sunrise and the sunsetting there had not been found his equal. And now, poor fool, I know that there was never any man like this!"

"Nay, there was such a man," the poet said, "in an old time which I almost forget. To-day he is quite dead. There is only a poor wretch who has been faithless in all things, who has not even served the devil faithfully."

"Why, then, you lackey with a lackey's soul, attend to what I say. Can you make any terms with Umfraville?"

"I can do nothing," Ufford replied. "You have robbed him--as me--of what he most desired. You have made him the laughing-stock of England. He does not pardon any more than I would pardon."

"And as God lives and reigns, I do not greatly blame him," said young Calverley. "This man at least was wronged. Concerning you I do not speak, because of a false dream I had once very long ago. Yet Umfraville was treated infamously. I dare concede what I could not permit another man to say and live, now that I drink a toast which I must drink alone. For I drink to the honor of the Calverleys. I have not ever lied to any person in this world, and so I may not drink with you."

"Oh, but you drink because you know your death to be the one event which can insure her happiness," cried Ufford. "We are not much unlike. And I dare say it is only an imaginary Honoria we love, after all. Yet, look, my fellow-Ixion! for to the eye at least is she not perfect?"

The two men gazed for a long while. Amid that coterie of exquisites, wherein allusion to whatever might be ugly in the world was tacitly allowed to be unmentionable, Lady Honoria glitteringly went about the moment's mirthful business with lovely ardor. You saw now unmistakably that "Light Queen of Elfdom, dead Titania's heir" of whom Ufford writes in the fourth Satire. Honoria's prettiness, rouged, frail, and modishly enhanced, allured the eye from all less elfin brilliancies; and as she laughed among so many other relishers of life her charms became the more instant, just as a painting quickens in every tint when set in an appropriate frame.

"There is no other way," her husband said. He drank and toasted what was dearest in the world, smiling to think how death came to him in that wine's familiar taste. "I drink to the most lovely of created ladies! and to her happiness!"

He snapped the stem of the glass and tossed it joyously aside.

"Assuredly, there is no other way," said Ufford. "And armored by that knowledge, even I may drink as honorable people do. Pro honoria!" Then this man also broke his emptied glass.

"How long have I to live?" said Calverley, and took snuff.

"Why, thirty years, I think, unless you duel too immoderately," replied Lord Ufford,--"since while you looked at Honoria I changed our glasses. No! no! a thing done has an end. Besides, it is not unworthy of me. So go boldly to the Earl of Bute and tell him all. You are my cousin and my successor. Yes, very soon you, too, will be a peer of England and as safe from molestation as is Lord Pevensey. I am the first to tender my congratulations. Now I make certain that they are not premature."

The poet laughed at this moment as a man may laugh in hell. He reeled. His lean face momentarily contorted, and afterward the poet died.

"I am Lord Ufford," said Calverley aloud. "The person of a peer is inviolable----" He presently looked downward from rapt gazing at his wife.

Fresh from this horrible half-hour, he faced a future so alluring as by its beauty to intimidate him. Youth, love, long years of happiness, and (by this capricious turn) now even opulence, were the ingredients of a captivating vista. And yet he needs must pause a while to think of the dear comrade he had lost--of that loved boy, his pattern in the time of their common youthfulness which gleamed in memory as bright and misty as a legend, and of the perfect chevalier who had been like a touchstone to Robert Calverley a bare half-hour ago. He knelt, touched lightly the fallen jaw, and lightly kissed the cheek of this poor wreckage; and was aware that the caress was given with more tenderness than Robert Calverley had shown in the same act a bare half-hour ago.

Meanwhile the music of a country dance urged the new Earl of Ufford to come and frolic where every one was laughing; and to partake with gusto of the benefits which chance had provided; and to be forthwith as merry as was decorous in a peer of England.

THE IRRESISTIBLE OGLE

But after SHERIDAN had risen to a commanding position in the gay life of London, he rather disliked to be known as a playwright or a poet, and preferred to be regarded as a statesman and a man of fashion who 'set the pace' in all pastimes of the opulent and idle. Yet, whatever he really thought of his own writings, and whether or not he did them, as Stevenson used to say, 'just for fun,' the fact remains that he was easily the most distinguished and brilliant dramatist of an age which produced in SHERIDAN'S solemn vagaries one of its most characteristic products."

Look on this form,--where humor, quaint and sly,
Dimples the cheek, and points the beaming eye;
Where gay invention seems to boast its wiles
In amorous hint, and half-triumphant smiles.

Look on her well--does she seem form'd to teach?
Should you expect to hear this lady preach?
Is gray experience suited to her youth?
Do solemn sentiments become that mouth?

Bid her be grave, those lips should rebel prove
To every theme that slanders mirth or love.

RICHARD BRINSLEY SHERIDAN.--Second Prologue to The Rivals.

THE IRRESISTIBLE OGLE

The devotion of Mr. Sheridan to the Dean of Winchester's daughter, Miss Esther Jane Ogle--or "the irresistible Ogle," as she was toasted at the Kit-cat--was now a circumstance to be assumed in the polite world of London. As a result, when the parliamentarian followed her into Scotland, in the spring of 1795, people only shrugged.

"Because it proves that misery loves company," was Mr. Fox's observation at Wattier's, hard upon two in the morning. "Poor Sherry, as an inconsolable widower, must naturally have some one to share his grief. He perfectly comprehends that no one will lament the death of his wife more fervently than her successor."

In London Mr. Fox thus worded his interpretation of the matter; and spoke, oddly enough, at the very moment that in Edinburgh Mr. Sheridan returned to his lodgings in Abercromby Place, deep in the reminiscences of a fortunate evening at cards. In consequence, Mr. Sheridan entered the room so quietly that the young man who was employed in turning over the contents of the top bureau-drawer was taken unprepared.

But in the marauder's nature, as far as resolution went, was little lacking. "Silence!" he ordered, and with the mandate a pistol was leveled upon the representative for the borough of Stafford. "One cry for help, and you perish like a dog. I warn you that I am a desperate man."

"Now, even at a hazard of discourtesy, I must make bold to question your statement," said Mr. Sheridan, "although, indeed, it is not so much the recklessness as the masculinity which I dare call into dispute."

He continued, in his best parliamentary manner, a happy blending of reproach, omniscience and pardon. "Only two months ago," said Mr. Sheridan, "I was so fortunate as to encounter a lady who, alike through the attractions of her person and the sprightliness of her conversation, convinced me I was on the road to fall in love after the high fashion of a popular romance. I accordingly make her a declaration. I am rejected. I besiege her with the customary artillery of sonnets, bouquets, serenades, bonbons, theater-tickets and threats of suicide. In fine, I contract the habit of proposing to Miss Ogle on every Wednesday; and so strong is my infatuation that I follow her as far into the north as Edinburgh in order to secure my eleventh rejection at half-past ten last evening."

"I fail to understand," remarked the burglar, "how all this prolix account of your amours can possibly concern me."

"You are at least somewhat involved in the deplorable climax," Mr. Sheridan returned. "For behold! at two in the morning I discover the object of my adoration and the daughter of an estimable prelate, most calumniously clad and busily employed in rumpling my supply of cravats. If ever any lover was thrust into a more ambiguous position, madam, historians have touched on his dilemma with marked reticence."

He saw--and he admired--the flush which mounted to his visitor's brow. And then, "I must concede that appearances are against me, Mr. Sheridan," the beautiful intruder said. "And I hasten to protest that my presence in your apartments at this hour is prompted by no unworthy motive. I merely came to steal the famous diamond which you brought from London--the Honor of Eiran."

"Incomparable Esther Jane," ran Mr. Sheridan's answer, "that stone is now part of a brooch which was this afternoon returned to my cousin's, the Earl of Eiran's, hunting-lodge near Melrose. He intends the gem which you are vainly seeking among my haberdashery to be the adornment of his promised bride in the ensuing June. I confess to no overwhelming admiration as concerns this raucous if meritorious young person; and will even concede that the thought of her becoming my kinswoman rouses in me an inevitable distaste, no less attributable to the discord of her features than to the source of her eligibility to disfigure the peerage--that being her father's lucrative transactions in Pork, which I find indigestible in any form."

"A truce to paltering!" Miss Ogle cried. "That jewel was stolen from the temple at Moorshedabad, by the Earl of Eiran's grandfather, during the confusion necessarily attendant on the glorious battle of Plassy." She laid down the pistol, and resumed in milder tones: "From an age-long existence as the left eye of Ganesh it was thus converted into the loot of an invader. To restore this diamond to its lawful, although no doubt polygamous and inefficiently-attired proprietors is at this date impossible. But, oh! what claim have you to its possession?"

"Why, none whatever," said the parliamentarian; "and to contend as much would be the apex of unreason. For this diamond belongs, of course, to my cousin the Earl of Eiran----"

"As a thief's legacy!" She spoke with signs of irritation.

"Eh, eh, you go too fast! Eiran, to do him justice, is not a graduate in peculation. At worst, he is only the sort of fool one's cousins ordinarily are."

The trousered lady walked to and fro for a while, with the impatience of a caged lioness. "I perceive I must go more deeply into matters," Miss Ogle remarked, and, with that habitual gesture which he fondly recognized, brushed back a straying lock of hair. "In any event," she continued, "you cannot with reason deny that the world's wealth is inequitably distributed?"

"Madam," Mr. Sheridan returned, "as a member of Parliament, I have necessarily made it a rule never to understand political economy. It is as apt as not to prove you are selling your vote to the wrong side of the House, and that hurts one's conscience."

"Ah, that is because you are a man. Men are not practical. None of you has ever dared to insist on his opinion about anything until he had secured the cowardly corroboration of a fact or so to endorse him. It is a pity. Yet, since through no fault of yours your sex is invariably misled by its hallucinations as to the importance of being rational, I will refrain from logic and statistics. In a word, I simply inform you that I am a member of the League of Philanthropic Larcenists."

"I had not previously heard of this organization," said Mr. Sheridan, and not without suspecting his response to be a masterpiece in the inadequate.

"Our object is the benefit of society at large," Miss Ogle explained; "and our obstacles so far have been, in chief, the fetish of proprietary rights and the ubiquity of the police."

And with that she seated herself and told him of the league's inception by a handful of reflective persons, admirers of Rousseau and converts to his tenets, who were resolved to better the circumstances of the indigent. With amiable ardor Miss Ogle explained how from the petit larcenies of charity-balls and personally solicited subscriptions the league had mounted to an ampler field of depredation; and through what means it now took toll from every form of wealth unrighteously acquired. Divertingly she described her personal experiences in the separation of usurers, thieves, financiers, hereditary noblemen, popular authors, and other social parasites, from the ill-got profits of their disreputable vocations. And her account of how, on the preceding Tuesday, she, single-handed, had robbed Sir Alexander McRae--who then enjoyed a fortune and an enviable reputation for philanthropy, thanks to the combination of glucose, vitriol and other chemicals which he prepared under the humorous pretext of manufacturing beer--wrung high encomiums from Mr. Sheridan.

"The proceeds of these endeavors," Miss Ogle added, "are conscientiously devoted to ameliorating the condition of meritorious paupers. I would be happy to submit to you our annual report. Then you may judge for yourself how many families we have snatched from the depths of poverty and habitual intoxication to the comparative comfort of a vine-embowered cottage."

Mr. Sheridan replied: "I have not ever known of any case where adoration needed an affidavit for foundation. Oh, no, incomparable Esther Jane! I am not in a position to be solaced by the reports of a corresponding secretary. I gave my heart long since; to-night I fling my confidence into the bargain; and am resolved to serve wholeheartedly the cause to which you are devoted. In consequence, I venture to propose my name for membership in the enterprise you advocate and indescribably adorn."

Miss Ogle was all one blush, such was the fervor of his utterance. "But first you must win your spurs, Mr. Sheridan. I confess you are not abhorrent to me," she hurried on, "for you are the most fascinatingly hideous man I have ever seen; and it was always the apprehension that you might look on burglary as an unmaidenly avocation which has compelled me to discourage your addresses. Now all is plain; and should you happen to distinguish yourself in robbery of the criminally opulent, you will have, I believe, no reason to complain of a twelfth refusal. I cannot modestly say more."

He laughed. "It is a bargain. We will agree that I bereave some person of either stolen or unearned property, say, to the value of L10,000----" And with his usual carefulness in such matters, Mr. Sheridan entered the wager in his notebook.

She yielded him her hand in token of assent. And he, depend upon it, kissed that velvet trifle fondly.

"And now," said Mr. Sheridan, "to-morrow we will visit Bemerside and obtain possession of that crystal which is in train to render me the happiest of men. The task will be an easy one, as Eiran is now in England, and his servants for the most part are my familiars."

"I agree to your proposal," she answered. "But this diamond is my allotted quarry; and any assistance you may render me in procuring it will not, of course, affect in any way our bargain. On this point"--she spoke with a break of laughter--"I am as headstrong as an allegory on the banks of the Nile."

"To quote an author to his face," lamented Mr. Sheridan, "is bribery as gross as it is efficacious. I must unwillingly consent to your exorbitant demands, for you are, as always, the irresistible Ogle."

Miss Ogle bowed her gratitude; and, declining Mr. Sheridan's escort, for fear of arousing gossip by being seen upon the street with him at this late hour, preferred to avoid any appearance of indecorum by climbing down the kitchen roof.

When she had gone, Mr. Sheridan very gallantly attempted a set of verses. But the Muse was not to be wooed to-night, and stayed obstinately coy.

Mr. Sheridan reflected, rather forlornly, that he wrote nothing nowadays. There was, of course, his great comedy, *Affectation*, his masterpiece which he meant to finish at one time or another; yet, at the bottom of his heart, he knew that he would never finish it. But, then, deuce take posterity! for to have written the best comedy, the best farce, and the best burlesque as well, that England had ever known, was a very prodigal wiping-out of every obligation toward posterity. Boys thought a deal about posterity, as he remembered; but a sensible man would bear in mind that all this world's delicacies--its merry diversions, its venison and old wines, its handsomely-bound books and fiery-hearted jewels and sumptuous clothings, all its lovely things that can be touched and handled, and more especially its ear-tickling applause--were to be won, if ever, from one's contemporaries. And people were generous toward social, rather than literary, talents for the sensible reason that they derived more pleasure from an agreeable companion at dinner than from having a rainy afternoon rendered endurable by some book or another. So the parliamentarian sensibly went to bed.

Miss Ogle during this Scottish trip was accompanied by her father, the venerable Dean of Winchester. The Dean, although in all things worthy of implicit confidence, was not next day informed of the intended expedition, in deference to public opinion, which, as Miss Ogle pointed out, regards a clergyman's participation in a technical felony with disapproval.

Miss Ogle, therefore, radiant in a becoming gown of pink lute-string, left Edinburgh the following morning under cover of a subterfuge, and with Mr. Sheridan as her only escort. He was at pains to adorn this role with so many happy touches of courtesy and amiability that their confinement in the postchaise appeared to both of incredible brevity.

When they had reached Melrose another chaise was ordered to convey them to Bemerside; and pending its forthcoming Mr. Sheridan and Miss Ogle strolled among the famous ruins of Melrose Abbey. The parliamentarian had caused his hair to be exuberantly curled that morning, and figured to advantage in a plum-colored coat and a saffron waistcoat sprigged with forget-me-nots. He chatted entertainingly concerning the Second Pointed style of architecture; translated many of the epitaphs; and was abundant in interesting information as to Robert Bruce, and Michael Scott, and the rencounter of Chevy Chase.

"Oh, but observe," said Mr. Sheridan, more lately, "our only covering is the dome of heaven. Yet in their time these aisles were populous, and here a score of generations have besought what earth does not afford--now where the banners of crusaders waved the ivy flutters, and there is no incense in this consecrated house except the breath of the wild rose."

"The moral is an old one," she returned. "Mummy is become merchandise, Mizraim cures wounds, and Pharaoh is sold for balsams."

"You are a reader, madam?" he observed, with some surprise; and he continued: "Indeed, my thoughts were on another trail. I was considering that the demolishers of this place--those English armies, those followers of John Knox--were actuated by the highest and most laudable of motives. As a result we find the house of Heaven converted into a dustheap."

"I believe you attempt an apologue," she said, indignantly. "Upon my word, I think you would insinuate that philanthropy, when forced to manifest itself through embezzlement, is a less womanly employment than the darning of stockings!"

"Whom the cap fits----" he answered, with a bow. "Indeed, incomparable Esther Jane, I had said nothing whatever touching hosiery; and it was equally remote from my intentions to set up as a milliner."

They lunched at Bemerside, where Mr. Sheridan was cordially received by the steward, and a well-chosen repast was placed at their disposal.

"Fergus," Mr. Sheridan observed, as they chatted over their dessert concerning famous gems--in which direction talk had been adroitly steered"--Fergus, since we are on the topic, I would like to show Miss Ogle the Honor of Eiran."

The Honor of Eiran was accordingly produced from a blue velvet case, and was properly admired. Then, when the steward had been dismissed to fetch a rare liqueur, Mr. Sheridan laughed, and tossed and caught the jewel, as though he handled a cricket-ball. It was the size of a pigeon's egg, and was set among eight gems of lesser magnitude; and in transit through the sunlight the trinket flashed and glittered with diabolical beauty. The parliamentarian placed three bits of sugar in the velvet case and handed the gem to his companion.

"The bulk is much the same," he observed; "and whether the carbon be crystallized or no, is the responsibility of stratigraphic geology. Fergus, perhaps, must go to jail. That is unfortunate. But true philanthropy works toward the benefit of the greatest number possible; and this resplendent pebble will purchase you innumerable pounds of tea and a warehouseful of blankets."

"But, Mr. Sheridan," Miss Ogle cried, in horror, "to take this brooch would not be honest!"

"Oh, as to that----!" he shrugged.

"----because Lord Eiran purchased all these lesser diamonds, and very possibly paid for them."

Then Mr. Sheridan reflected, stood abashed, and said: "Incomparable Esther Jane, I confess I am only a man. You are entirely right. To purloin any of these little diamonds would be an abominable action, whereas to make off with the only valuable one is simply a stroke of retribution. I will, therefore, attempt to prise it out with a nutpick."

Three constables came suddenly into the room. "We hae been tauld this missy is a suspectit thieving body," their leader cried. "Esther Jane Ogle, ye maun gae with us i' the law's name. Ou ay, lass, ye ken weel eneugh wha robbit auld Sir Aleexander McRae, sae dinna ye say naething tae your ain preejudice, lest ye hae tae account for it a'."

Mr. Sheridan rose to the occasion. "My exceedingly good friend, Angus Howden! I am unwilling to concede that yeomen can excel in gentlemanly accomplishments, but it is only charity to suppose all three of you as drunk as any duke that ever honored me with his acquaintance." This he drawled, and appeared magisterially to await an explanation.

"Hout, Mr. Sheridan," commenced the leading representative of justice, "let that flee stick i' the wa'--e dinna mean tae tell me, Sir, that ye are acquaintit wi' this--ou ay, tae pleasure ye, I micht e'en say wi' this----"

"This lady, probably?" Mr. Sheridan hazarded.

"'Tis an unco thing," the constable declared, "but that wad be the word was amaist at my tongue's tip."

"Why, undoubtedly," Mr. Sheridan assented. "I rejoice that, being of French extraction, and unconversant with your somewhat cryptic patois, the lady in question is the less likely to have been sickened by your extravagances in the way of misapprehension. I candidly confess such imbecility annoys me. What!" he cried out, "what if I marry! is matrimony to be ranked with arson? And what if my cousin, Eiran, affords me a hiding-place wherein to sneak through our honeymoon after the cowardly fashion of all modern married couples! Am I in consequence compelled to submit to the invasions of an intoxicated constabulary?" His rage was terrific.

"Voila la seule devise. Ils me connaissent, ils ont confidence dans moi. Si, taisez-vous! Si non, vous serez arretee et mise dans la prison, comme une caractere suspicieuse!" Mr. Sheridan exhorted Miss Ogle to this intent with more of earnestness than linguistic perfection; and he rejoiced to see that instantly she caught at her one chance of plausibly accounting for her presence at Bemerside, and of effecting a rescue from this horrid situation.

"But I also spik the English," she sprightlily announced. "I am appleed myself at to learn its by heart. Certainly you look for a needle in a hay bundle, my gentlemans. I am no stealer of the grand road, but the wife of Mistaire Sheridan, and her presence will say to you the remains."

"You see!" cried Mr. Sheridan, in modest triumph. "In short, I am a bridegroom unwarrantably interrupted in his first *tete-a-tete*, I am responsible for this lady and all her past and its appurtenances; and, in a phrase, for everything except the course of conduct I will undoubtedly pursue should you be visible at the conclusion of the next five minutes."

His emphasis was such that the police withdrew with a concomitant of apologies.

"And now I claim my bond," said Mr. Sheridan, when they were once again free from intrusion. "For we two are in Scotland, where the common declaration of a man and woman that they are married constitutes a marriage."

"Oh----!" she exclaimed, and stood encrimsoned.

"Indeed, I must confess that the day's work has been a trick throughout. The diamond was pawned years ago. This trinket here is a copy in paste and worth perhaps some seven shillings sixpence. And those fellows were not constables, but just my cousin Eiran and two footmen in disguise. Nay, madam, you will learn with experience that to display unfailing candor is not without exception the price of happiness."

"But this, I think, evades our bargain, Mr. Sheridan. For you were committed to pilfer property to the value of L10,000----"

"And to fulfil the obligation I have stolen your hand in marriage. What, madam! do you indeed pretend that any person outside of Bedlam would value you at less? Believe me, your perfections are of far more worth. All persons recognize that save yourself, incomparable Esther Jane; and yet, so patent is the proof of my contention, I dare to leave the verdict to your sense of justice."

Miss Ogle did not speak. Her lashes fell as, with some ceremony, he led her to the long French mirror which was in the breakfast room. "See now!" said Mr. Sheridan. "You, who endanger life and fame in order to provide a mendicant with gruel, tracts and blankets! You, who deny a sop to the one hunger which is vital! Oh, madam, I am tempted glibly to compare your eyes to sapphires, and your hair to thin-spun gold, and the color of your flesh to the arbutus-flower--for that, as you can see, would be within the truth, and it would please most women, and afterward they would not be so obdurate. But you are not like other women," Mr. Sheridan observed, with admirable dexterity. "And I aspire to you, the irresistible Ogle! you, who so great-heartedly befriend the beggar! you, who with such industry contrive alleviation for the discomforts of poverty. Eh, eh! what will you grant to any beggar such as I? Will you deny a sop to the one hunger which is vital?" He spoke with unaccustomed vigor, even in a sort of terror, because he knew that he was speaking with sincerity.

"To the one hunger which is vital!" he repeated. "Ah, where lies the secret which makes one face the dearest in the world, and entrusts to one little hand a life's happiness as a plaything? All Aristotle's learning could not unriddle the mystery, and Samson's thews were impotent to break that spell. Love vanquishes all. . . . You would remind me of some previous skirmishings with Venus's unconquerable brat? Nay, madam, to the contrary, the fact that I have loved many other women is my strongest plea for toleration. Were there nothing else, it is indisputable we perform all actions better for having rehearsed them. No, we do not of necessity perform them the more thoughtlessly as well; for, indeed, I find that with experience a man becomes increasingly difficult to please in affairs of the heart. The woman one loves then is granted that pre-eminence not merely by virtue of having outshone any particular one of her predecessors; oh, no! instead, her qualities have been compared with all the charms of all her fair forerunners, and they have endured that stringent testing. The winning of an often-bartered heart is in reality the only conquest which entitles a woman to complacency, for she has received a real compliment; whereas to be selected as the target of a lad's first declaration is a tribute of no more value than a man's opinion upon vintages who has never tasted wine."

He took a turn about the breakfast room, then came near to her. "I love you. Were there any way to parade the circumstance and bedeck it with pleasing adornments of filed phrases, tropes and far-fetched similes, I would not grudge you a deal of verbal pageantry. But three words say all. I love you. There is no act in my past life but appears trivial and strange to me, and to the man who performed it I seem no more akin than to Mark Antony or Nebuchadnezzar. I love you. The skies are bluer since you came, the beauty of this world we live in oppresses me with a fearful joy, and in my heart there is always the thought of you and such yearning as I may not word. For I love you."

"You--but you have frightened me." Miss Ogle did not seem so terrified as to make any effort to recede from him; and yet he saw that she was frightened in sober earnest. Her face showed pale, and soft, and glad, and awed, and desirable above all things; and it remained so near him as to engender riotous aspirations.

"I love you," he said again. You would never have suspected this man could speak, upon occasion, fluently. "I think--I think that Heaven was prodigal when

Heaven made you. To think of you is as if I listened to an exalted music; and to be with you is to understand that all imaginable sorrows are just the figments of a dream which I had very long ago."

She laid one hand on each of his shoulders, facing him. "Do not let me be too much afraid! I have not ever been afraid before. Oh, everything is in a mist of gold, and I am afraid of you, and of the big universe which I was born into, and I am helpless, and I would have nothing changed! Only, I cannot believe I am worth L10,000, and I do so want to be persuaded I am. It is a great pity," she sighed, "that you who convicted Warren Hastings of stealing such enormous wealth cannot be quite as eloquent to-day as you were in the Oudh speech, and convince me his arraigner has been equally rapacious!"

"I mean to prove as much--with time," said Mr. Sheridan. His breathing was yet perfunctory.

Miss Ogle murmured, "And how long would you require?"

"Why, I intend, with your permission, to devote the remainder of my existence to the task. Eh, I concede that space too brief for any adequate discussion of the topic; but I will try to be concise and very practical----"

She laughed. They were content. "Try, then----" Miss Ogle said.

She was able to get no farther in the sentence, for reasons which to particularize would be indiscreet.

A PRINCESS OF GRUB STREET

Though--or, rather, because--VANDERHOFFEN was a child of the French Revolution, and inherited his social, political and religious--or, rather, anti-religious--views from the French writers of the eighteenth century, England was not ready for him and the unshackled individualism for which he at first contended. Recognizing this fact, he turned to an order of writing begotten of the deepest popular needs and addressed to the best intelligence of the great middle classes of the community."

Now emperors bide their times' rebuff
I would not be a king--enough
   Of woe it is to love;
The paths of power are steep and rough,
   And tempests reign above.

I would not climb the imperial throne;
'Tis built on ice which fortune's sun
   Thaws in the height of noon.
Then farewell, kings, that squeak 'Ha' done!'
   To time's full-throated tune.

PAUL VANDERHOFFEN.--Emma and Caroline.

A PRINCESS OF GRUB STREET

It is questionable if the announcement of the death of their Crown Prince, Hilary, upon the verge of his accession to the throne, aroused more than genteel regret among the inhabitants of Saxe-Kesselberg. It is indisputable that in diplomatic circles news of this horrible occurrence was indirectly conceded in 1803 to smack of a direct intervention of Providence. For to consider all the havoc dead Prince Fribble--such had been his sobriquet--would have created, ***Dei gratia***, through his pilotage of an important grand-duchy (with an area of no less than eighty-nine square miles) was less discomfortable now prediction was an academic matter.

And so the editors of divers papers were the victims of a decorous anguish, court-mourning was decreed, and that wreckage which passed for the mutilated body of Prince Hilary was buried with every appropriate honor. Within the week most people had forgotten him, for everybody was discussing the execution of the Duc d'Enghein. And the aged unvenerable Grand-Duke of Saxe-Kesselberg died too in the same March; and afterward his other grandson, Prince Augustus, reigned in the merry old debauchee's stead.

Prince Hilary was vastly pleased. His scheme for evading the tedious responsibilities of sovereignty had been executed without a hitch; he was officially dead; and, on the whole, standing bareheaded between a miller and laundress, he had found his funeral ceremonies to be unimpeachably conducted. He assumed the name of Paul Vanderhoffen, selected at random from the novel he was reading when his postchaise conveyed him past the frontier of Saxe-Kesselberg. Freed, penniless, and thoroughly content, he set about amusing himself--having a world to frisk in--and incidentally about the furnishing of his new friend Paul Vanderhoffen with life's necessaries.

It was a little more than two years later that the good-natured Earl of Brudenel suggested to Lady John Claridge that she could nowhere find a more eligible tutor for her son than young Vanderhoffen.

"Hasn't a shilling, ma'am, but one of the most popular men in London. His poetry book was subscribed for by the Prince Regent and half the notables of the kingdom.   Capital company at a dinner-table--stutters, begad, like a What-you-may-call-'em, and keeps everybody in a roar--and when he's had his whack of claret, he sings his own songs to the piano, you know, and all that sort of thing, and has quite put Tommy Moore's nose out of joint. Nobody knows much about him, but that don't matter with these literary chaps, does it now? Goes everywhere, ma'am--quite a favorite at Carlton House--a highly agreeable, well-informed man, I can assure you--and probably hasn't a shilling to pay the cabman. Deuced odd, ain't it? But Lord Lansdowne is trying to get him a place--spoke to me about a tutorship, ma'am, in fact, just to keep Vanderhoffen going, until some registrarship or other falls vacant. Now, I ain't clever and that sort of thing, but I quite agree with Lansdowne that we practical men ought to look out for these clever fellows--see that they don't starve in a garret, like poor What's-his-name, don't you know?"

Lady Claridge sweetly agreed with her future son-in-law. So it befell that shortly after this conversation Paul Vanderhoffen came to Leamington Manor, and through an entire summer goaded young Percival Claridge, then on the point of entering Cambridge, but pedagogically branded as "deficient in mathematics," through many elaborate combinations of x and y and cosines and hyperbolas.

Lady John Claridge, mother to the pupil, approved of the new tutor. True, he talked much and wildishly; but literary men had a name for eccentricity, and, besides, Lady Claridge always dealt with the opinions of other people as matters of illimitable unimportance. This baronet's lady, in short, was in these days vouchsafing to the universe at large a fine and new benevolence, now that her daughter was safely engaged to Lord Brudenel, who, whatever his other virtues, was certainly a peer of England and very rich. It seems irrelevant, and yet for the tale's sake is noteworthy, that any room which harbored Lady John Claridge was through this fact converted into an absolute monarchy.

And so, by the favor of Lady Claridge and destiny, the tutor stayed at Leamington Manor all summer.

There was nothing in either the appearance or demeanor of the fiancee of Lord Brudenel's title and superabundant wealth which any honest gentleman could, hand upon his heart, describe as blatantly repulsive.

It may not be denied the tutor noted this. In fine, he fell in love with Mildred Claridge after a thorough-going fashion such as Prince Fribble would have found amusing. Prince Fribble would have smiled, shrugged, drawled, "Eh, after all, the girl is handsome and deplorably cold-blooded!" Paul Vanderhoffen said, "I am not fit to live in the same world with her," and wrote many verses in the prevailing Oriental style rich in allusions to roses, and bulbuls, and gazelles, and peris, and minarets--which he sold rather profitably.

Meanwhile, far oversea, the reigning Duke of Saxe-Kesselberg had been unwise enough to quarrel with his Chancellor, Georges Desmarets, an invaluable man whose only faults were dishonesty and a too intimate acquaintance with the circumstances of Prince Hilary's demise. As fruit of this indiscretion, an inconsiderable tutor at Leamington Manor--whom Lady John Claridge regarded as a sort of upper servant was talking with a visitor.

The tutor, it appeared, preferred to talk with the former Chancellor of Saxe-Kesselberg in the middle of an open field. The time was afternoon, the season September, and the west was vaingloriously justifying the younger man's analogy of a gigantic Spanish omelette. Meanwhile, the younger man declaimed in a high-pitched pleasant voice, wherein there was, as always, the elusive suggestion of a stutter.

"I repeat to you," the tutor observed, "that no consideration will ever make a grand-duke of me excepting over my dead body. Why don't you recommend some not quite obsolete vocation, such as making papyrus, or writing an interesting novel, or teaching people how to dance a saraband? For after all, what is a monarch nowadays--oh, even a monarch of the first class?" he argued, with what came near being a squeak of indignation. "The poor man is a rather pitiable and perfectly useless relic of barbarism, now that 1789 has opened our eyes; and his main business in life is to ride in open carriages and bow to an applauding public who are applauding at so much per head. He must expect to be aspersed with calumny, and once in a while with bullets. He may at the utmost aspire to introduce an innovation in evening dress,--the Prince Regent, for instance, has invented a really very creditable shoe-buckle. Tradition obligates him to devote his unofficial hours to sheer depravity----"

Paul Vanderhoffen paused to meditate.

"Why, there you are! another obstacle! I have in an inquiring spirit and without prejudice sampled all the Seven Deadly Sins, and the common increment was an inability to enjoy my breakfast. A grand-duke I take it, if he have any sense of the responsibilities of his position, will piously remember the adage about the voice of the people and hasten to be steeped in vice--and thus conform to every popular notion concerning a grand-duke. Why, common intelligence demands that a grand-duke should brazenly misbehave himself upon the more conspicuous high-places of Chemosh! and personally, I have no talents such as would qualify me for a life of cynical and brutal immorality. I lack the necessary aptitude, I would not ever afford any spicy gossip concerning the Duke of Saxe-Kesselberg, and the editors of the society papers would unanimously conspire to dethrone me----"

Thus he argued, with his high-pitched pleasant voice, wherein there was, as always, the elusive suggestion of a stutter. And here the other interrupted.

"There is no need of names, your highness." Georges Desmarets was diminutive, black-haired and corpulent. He was of dapper appearance, point-device in everything, and he reminded you of a perky robin.

The tutor flung out an "Ouf! I must recall to you that, thank heaven, I am not anybody's highness any longer. I am Paul Vanderhoffen."

"He says that he is not Prince Fribble!"--the little man addressed the zenith--"as if any other person ever succeeded in talking a half-hour without being betrayed into at least one sensible remark. Oh, how do you manage without fail to be so consistently and stupendously idiotic?"

"It is, like all other desirable traits, either innate or else just unattainable," the other answered. "I am so hopelessly light-minded that I cannot refrain from being rational even in matters which concern me personally--and this, of course, no normal being ever thinks of doing. I really cannot help it."

The Frenchman groaned whole-heartedly.

"But we were speaking--well, of foreign countries. Now, Paul Vanderhoffen has read that in one of these countries there was once a prince who very narrowly escaped figuring as a self-conscious absurdity, as an anachronism, as a life-long prisoner of etiquette. However, with the assistance of his cousin--who, incidentally, was also his heir--the prince most opportunely died. Oh, pedant that you are! in any event he was interred. And so, the prince was gathered to his fathers, and his cousin Augustus reigned in his stead. Until a certain politician who had been privy to this pious fraud----" The tutor shrugged. "How can I word it without seeming hypercritical?"

Georges Desmarets stretched out appealing hands. "But, I protest, it was the narrow-mindedness of that pernicious prig, your cousin--who firmly believes himself to be an improved and augmented edition of the Four Evangelists----"

"Well, in any event, the proverb was attested that birds of a feather make strange bedfellows. There was a dispute concerning some petit larceny--some slight discrepancy, we will imagine, since all this is pure romance, in the politician's accounts----"

"Now you belie me----" said the black-haired man, and warmly.

"Oh, Desmarets, you are as vain as ever! Let us say, then, of grand larceny. In any event, the politician was dismissed. And what, my dears, do you suppose this bold and bad and unprincipled Machiavelli went and did? Why, he made straight for the father of the princess the usurping duke was going to marry, and surprised everybody by showing that, at a pinch, even this Guy Fawkes--who was stuffed with all manner of guile and wickedness where youthful patriotism would ordinarily incline to straw--was capable of telling the truth. And so the father broke off the match. And the enamored, if usurping, duke wept bitterly and tore his hair to such an extent he totally destroyed his best toupet. And privily the Guy Fawkes came into the presence of the exiled duke and prated of a restoration to ancestral dignities. And he was spurned by a certain highly intelligent person who considered it both tedious and ridiculous to play at being emperor of a backyard. And then--I really don't recall what happened. But there was a general and unqualified deuce to pay with no pitch at a really satisfying temperature."

The stouter man said quietly: "It is a thrilling tale which you narrate. Only, I do recall what happened then. The usurping duke was very much in earnest, desirous of retaining his little kingdom, and particularly desirous of the woman whom he loved. In consequence, he had Monsieur the Runaway obliterated while the latter was talking nonsense----"

The tutor's brows had mounted.

"I scorn to think it even of anybody who is controlled in every action by a sense of duty," Georges Desmarets explained, "that Duke Augustus would cause you to be murdered in your sleep."

"A hit!" The younger man unsmilingly gesticulated like one who has been touched in sword-play. "Behold now, as the populace in their blunt way would phrase it, I am squelched."

"And so the usurping duke was married and lived happily ever afterward." Georges Desmarets continued: "I repeat to you there is only the choice between declaring yourself and being--we will say, removed. Your cousin is deeply in love with the Princess Sophia, and thanks to me, has now no chance of marrying her until his title has been secured by your--removal. Do not deceive yourself. High interests are involved. You are the grain of sand between big wheels. I iterate that the footpad who attacked you last night was merely a prologue. I happen to know your cousin has entrusted the affair to Heinrich Obendorf, his foster-brother, who, as you will remember, is not particularly squeamish."

Paul Vanderhoffen thought a while. "Desmarets," he said at last, "it is no use. I scorn your pribbles and your prabbles. I bargained with Augustus. I traded a duchy for my personal liberty. Frankly, I would be sorry to connect a sharer of my blood with the assault of yesterday. To be unpardonably candid, I have not ever found that your assertion of an event quite proved it had gone through the formality of occurring. And so I shall hold to my bargain."

"The night brings counsel," Desmarets returned. "It hardly needs a night, I think, to demonstrate that all I say is true."

And so they parted.

Having thus dismissed such trifles as statecraft and the well-being of empires, Paul Vanderhoffen turned toward consideration of the one really serious subject in the universe, which was of course the bright, miraculous and incredible perfection of Mildred Claridge.

"I wonder what you think of me? I wonder if you ever think of me?" The thought careered like a caged squirrel, now that he walked through autumn woods toward her home.

"I wish that you were not so sensible. I wish your mother were not even more so. The woman reeks with common-sense, and knows that to be common is to be unanswerable. I wish that a dispute with her were not upon a par with remonstrance against an earthquake."

He lighted a fresh cheroot. "And so you are to marry the Brudenel title and bank account, with this particular Heleigh thrown in as a dividend. And why not?

the estate is considerable; the man who encumbers it is sincere in his adoration of you; and, chief of all, Lady John Claridge has decreed it. And your decision in any matter has always lain between the claws of that steel-armored crocodile who, by some miracle, is your mother. Oh, what a universe! were I of hasty temperament I would cry out, TUT AND GO TO!"

This was the moment which the man hid in the thicket selected as most fit for intervention through the assistance of a dueling pistol. Paul Vanderhoffen reeled, his face bewilderment. His hands clutched toward the sky, as if in anguish he grasped at some invisible support, and he coughed once or twice. It was rather horrible. Then Vanderhoffen shivered as though he were very cold, and tottered and collapsed in the parched roadway.

A slinking man whose lips were gray and could not refrain from twitching came toward the limp heap. "So----!" said the man. One of his hands went to the tutor's breast, and in his left hand dangled a second dueling pistol. He had thrown away the other after firing it.

"And so----!" observed Paul Vanderhoffen. Afterward there was a momentary tussle. Now Paul Vanderhoffen stood erect and flourished the loaded pistol. "If you go on this way," he said, with some severity, "you will presently be neither loved nor respected. There was a time, though, when you were an excellent shot, Herr Heinrich Obendorf."

"I had my orders, highness," said the other stolidly.

"Oh yes, of course," Paul Vanderhoffen answered. "You had your orders--from Augustus!" He seemed to think of something very far away. He smiled, with quizzically narrowed eyes such as you may yet see in Raeburn's portrait of the man. "I was remembering, oddly enough, that elm just back of the Canova Pavilion--as it was twenty years ago. I managed to scramble up it, but Augustus could not follow me because he had such short fat little legs. He was so proud of what I had done that he insisted on telling everybody--and afterward we had oranges for luncheon, I remember, and sucked them through bits of sugar. It is not fair that you must always remember and always love that boy who played with you when you were little--after he has grown up to be another person. Eh no! youth passes, but all its memories of unimportant things remain with you and are less kind than any self-respecting viper would be. Decidedly, it is not fair, and some earnest-minded person ought to write to his morning paper about it. . . . I think that is the reason I am being a sentimental fool," Paul Vanderhoffen explained.

Then his teeth clicked. "Get on, my man," he said. "Do not remain too near to me, because there was a time when I loved your employer quite as much as you do. This fact is urging me to dangerous ends. Yes, it is prompting me, even while I talk with you, to give you a lesson in marksmanship, my inconveniently faithful Heinrich."

He shrugged. He lighted a cheroot with hands whose tremblings, he devoutly hoped, were not apparent, for Prince Fribble had been ashamed to manifest a sincere emotion of any sort, and Paul Vanderhoffen shared as yet this foible.

"Oh Brutus! Ravaillac! Damiens!" he drawled. "O general compendium of misguided aspirations! do be a duck and get along with you. And I would run as hard as I could, if I were you, for it is war now, and you and I are not on the same side."

Paul Vanderhoffen paused a hundred yards or so from this to shake his head. "Come, come! I have lost so much that I cannot afford to throw my good temper into the bargain. To endure with a grave face this perfectly unreasonable universe wherein destiny has locked me is undoubtedly meritorious; but to bustle about it like a caged canary, and not ever to falter in your hilarity, is heroic. Let us, by all means, not consider the obdurate if gilded barriers, but rather the lettuce and the cuttle-bone. I have my choice between becoming a corpse or a convict--a convict? ah, undoubtedly a convict, sentenced to serve out a life-term in a cess-pool of castby superstitions."

He smiled now over Paul Vanderhoffen's rage. "Since the situation is tragic, let us approach it in an appropriate spirit of frivolity. My circumstances bully me. And I succumb to irrationality, as rational persons invariably end by doing. But, oh, dear me! oh, Osiris, Termagaunt, and Zeus! to think there are at least a dozen other ne'er-do-wells alive who would prefer to make a mess of living as a grand-duke rather than as a scribbler in Grub Street! Well, well! the jest is not of my contriving, and the one concession a sane man will never yield the universe is that of considering it seriously."

And he strode on, resolved to be Prince Fribble to the last.

"Frivolity," he said, "is the smoked glass through which a civilized person views the only world he has to live in. For, otherwise, he could not presume to look upon such coruscations of insanity and remain unblinded."

This heartened him, as a rounded phrase will do the best of us. But by-and-bye,

"Frivolity," he groaned, "is really the cheap mask incompetence claps on when haled before a mirror."

And at Leamington Manor he found her strolling upon the lawn. It was an ordered, lovely scene, steeped now in the tranquillity of evening. Above, the stars were losing diffidence. Below, and within arms' reach, Mildred Claridge was treading the same planet on which he fidgeted and stuttered.

Something in his heart snapped like a fiddle-string, and he was entirely aware of this circumstance. As to her eyes, teeth, coloring, complexion, brows, height and hair, it is needless to expatiate. The most painstaking inventory of these chattels would necessarily be misleading, because the impression which they conveyed to him was that of a bewildering, but not distasteful, transfiguration of the universe, apt as a fanfare at the entrance of a queen.

But he would be Prince Fribble to the last. And so, "Wait just a moment, please," he said, "I want to harrow up your soul and freeze your blood."

Wherewith he suavely told her everything about Paul Vanderhoffen's origin and the alternatives now offered him, and she listened without comment.

"Ai! ai!" young Vanderhoffen perorated; "the situation is complete. I have not the least desire to be Grand-Duke of Saxe-Kesselberg. It is too abominably tedious. But, if I do not join in with Desmarets, who has the guy-ropes of a restoration well in hand, I must inevitably be--removed, as the knave phrases it. For as long as I live, I will be an insuperable barrier between Augustus and his Sophia. Otototoi!" he wailed, with a fine tone of tragedy, "the one impossible achievement in my life has always been to convince anybody that it was mine to dispose of as I elected!"

"Oh, man proposes----" she began, cryptically. Then he deliberated, and sulkily submitted: "But I may not even propose to abdicate. Augustus has put himself upon sworn record as an eye-witness of my hideous death. And in consequence I might keep on abdicating from now to the crack of doom, and the only course left open to him would be to treat me as an impostor."

She replied, with emphasis, "I think your cousin is a beast!"

"Ah, but the madman is in love," he pleaded. "You should not judge poor masculinity in such a state by any ordinary standards. Oh really, you don't know the Princess Sophia. She is, in sober truth, the nicest person who was ever born a princess. Why, she had actually made a mock of even that handicap, for ordinarily it is as disastrous to feminine appearance as writing books. And, oh, Lord! they will be marrying her to me, if Desmarets and I win out." Thus he forlornly ended.

"The designing minx!" Miss Claridge said, distinctly.

"Now, gracious lady, do be just a cooing pigeon and grant that when men are in love they are not any more encumbered by abstract notions about honor than if they had been womanly from birth. Come, let's be lyrical and open-minded," he urged; and he added, "No, either you are in love or else you are not in love. And nothing else will matter either way. You see, if men and women had been primarily designed to be rational creatures, there would be no explanation for their being permitted to continue in existence," he lucidly explained. "And to have grasped this fact is the pith of all wisdom."

"Oh, I am very wise." A glint of laughter shone in her eyes. "I would claim to be another Pythoness if only it did not sound so snaky and wriggling. So, from my trident--or was it a Triton they used to stand on?--I announce that you and your Augustus are worrying yourselves gray-headed over an idiotically simple problem. Now, I disposed of it offhand when I said, 'Man proposes.'"

He seemed to be aware of some one who from a considerable distance was inquiring her reasons for this statement.

"Because in Saxe-Kesselberg, as in all other German states, when a prince of the reigning house marries outside of the mediatized nobility he thereby forfeits his right of succession. It has been done any number of times. Why, don't you see, Mr. Vanderhoffen? Conceding you ever do such a thing, your cousin Augustus would become at once the legal heir. So you must marry. It is the only way, I think, to save you from regal incarceration and at the same time to reassure the Prince of Lueminster--that creature's father--that you have not, and never can have, any claim which would hold good in law. Then Duke Augustus could peaceably espouse his Sophia and go on reigning---- And, by the way, I have seen her picture often, and if that is what you call beauty----" Miss Claridge did not speak this last at least with any air of pointing out the self-evident.

And, "I believe," he replied, "that all this is actually happening. I might have known fate meant to glut her taste for irony."

"But don't you see? You have only to marry anybody outside of the higher nobility--and just as a makeshift----" She had drawn closer in the urgency of her desire to help him. An infinite despair and mirth as well was kindled by her nearness. And the man was insane and dimly knew as much.

And so, "I see," he answered. "But, as it happens, I cannot marry any woman, because I love a particular woman. At least, I suppose she isn't anything but just a woman. That statement," he announced, "is a formal tribute paid by what I call my intellect to what the vulgar call the probabilities. The rest of me has no patience whatever with such idiotic blasphemy."

She said, "I think I understand." And this surprised him, coming as it did from her whom he had always supposed to be the fiancee of Lord Brudenel's title and bank-account.

"And, well!"--he waved his hands--"either as tutor or as grand-duke, this woman is unattainable, because she has been far too carefully reared"--and here he frenziedly thought of that terrible matron whom, as you know, he had irreverently likened to a crocodile--"either to marry a pauper or to be contented with a left-handed alliance. And I love her. And so"--he shrugged--"there is positively nothing left to do save sit upon the ground and tell sad stories of the deaths of kings."

She said, "Oh, and you mean it! You are speaking the plain truth!" A change had come into her lovely face which would have made him think it even lovelier had not that contingency been beyond conception.

And Mildred Claridge said, "It is not fair for dreamers such as you to let a woman know just how he loves her. That is not wooing. It is bullying."

His lips were making a variety of irrational noises. And he was near to her. Also he realized that he had never known how close akin were fear and joy, so close the two could mingle thus, and be quite undistinguishable. And then repentance smote him.

"I am contemptible!" he groaned. "I had no right to trouble you with my insanities. Indeed I had not ever meant to let you guess how mad I was. But always I have evaded my responsibilities. So I remain Prince Fribble to the last."

"Oh, but I knew, I have always known." She held her eyes away from him. "And

I wrote to Lord Brudenel only yesterday releasing him from his engagement."

And now without uncertainty or haste Paul Vanderhoffen touched her cheek and raised her face, so that he saw it plainly in the rising twilight, and all its wealth of tenderness newborn. And what he saw there frightened him.

For the girl loved him! He felt himself to be, as most men do, a swindler when he comprehended this preposterous fact; and, in addition, he thought of divers happenings, such as shipwrecks, holocausts and earthquakes, which might conceivably have appalled him, and understood that he would never in his life face any sense of terror as huge as was this present sweet and illimitable awe.

And then he said, "You know that what I hunger for is impossible. There are so many little things, like common-sense, to be considered. For this is just a matter which concerns you and Paul Vanderhoffen--a literary hack, a stuttering squeak-voiced ne'er-do-well, with an acquired knack for scribbling verses that are feeble-minded enough for Annuals and Keepsake Books, and so fetch him an occasional guinea. For, my dear, the verses I write of my own accord are not sufficiently genteel to be vended in Paternoster Row; they smack too dangerously of human intelligence. So I am compelled, perforce, to scribble such jingles as I am ashamed to read, because I must write *something*. . . ." Paul Vanderhoffen shrugged, and continued, in tones more animated: "There will be no talk of any grand-duke. Instead, there will be columns of denunciation and tittle-tattle in every newspaper--quite as if you, a baronet's daughter, had run away with a footman. And you will very often think wistfully of Lord Brudenel's fine house when your only title is--well, Princess of Grub Street, and your realm is a garret. And for a while even to-morrow's breakfast will be a problematical affair. It is true Lord Lansdowne has promised me a registrarship in the Admiralty Court, and I do not think he will fail me. But that will give us barely enough to live on--with strict economy, which is a virtue that neither of us knows anything about. I beg you to remember that--you who have been used to every luxury! you who really were devised that you might stand beside an emperor and set tasks for him. In fine, you know----"

And Mildred Claridge said, "I know that, quite as I observed, man proposes--when he has been sufficiently prodded by some one who, because she is an idiot--And that is why I am not blushing--very much----"

"Your coloring is not--repellent." His high-pitched pleasant voice, in spite of him, shook now with more than its habitual suggestion of a stutter. "What have you done to me, my dear?" he said. "Why can't I jest at this . . . as I have always done at everything----?"

"Boy, boy!" she said; "laughter is excellent. And wisdom too is excellent. Only I think that you have laughed too much, and I have been too shrewd--But now I know that it is better to be a princess in Grub Street than to figure at Ranelagh as a good-hearted fool's latest purchase. For Lord Brudenel is really very good-natured," she argued, "and I did like him, and mother was so set upon it--and he was rich--and I honestly thought----"

"And now?" he said.

"And now I know," she answered happily.

They looked at each other for a little while. Then he took her hand, prepared in turn for self-denial.

"The **Household Review** wants me to 'do' a series on famous English bishops," he reported, humbly. "I had meant to refuse, because it would all have to be dull High-Church twaddle. And the **English Gentleman** wants some rather outrageous lying done in defense of the Corn Laws. You would not despise me too much-- would you, Mildred?--if I undertook it now. I really have no choice. And there is plenty of hackwork of that sort available to keep us going until more solvent days, when I shall have opportunity to write something quite worthy of you."

"For the present, dear, it would be much more sensible, I think, to 'do' the bishops and the Corn Laws. You see, that kind of thing pays very well, and is read by the best people; whereas poetry, of course-- But you can always come back to the verse-making, you know----"

"If you ever let me," he said, with a flash of prescience. "And I don't believe you mean to let me. You are your mother's daughter, after all! Nefarious woman, you are planning, already, to make a responsible member of society out of me! and you will do it, ruthlessly! Such is to be Prince Fribble's actual burial--in his own private carriage, with a receipted tax-bill in his pocket!"

"What nonsense you poets talk!" the girl observed. But to him, forebodingly, that familiar statement seemed to lack present application.

THE LADY OF ALL OUR DREAMS

In JOHN CHARTERIS appeared a man with an inborn sense of the supreme interest and the overwhelming emotional and spiritual relevancy of human life as it is actually and obscurely lived; a man with unmistakable creative impulses and potentialities; a man who, had he lived in a more mature and less self-deluding community--a community that did not so rigorously confine its interest in facts to business, and limit its demands upon art to the supplying of illusions--might humbly and patiently have schooled his gifts to the service of his vision. . . . As it was, he accepted defeat and compromised half-heartedly with commercialism."

> And men unborn will read of Heloise,
> And Ruth, and Rosamond, and Semele,
> When none remembers your name's melody
> Or rhymes your name, enregistered with these.
>
> And will my name wake moods as amorous
> As that of Abelard or Launcelot
> Arouses? be recalled when Pyramus
> And Tristram are unrhymed of and forgot?--
> Time's laughter answers, who accords to us
> More gracious fields, wherein we harvest--what?

JOHN CHARTERIS. *Torrismond's Envoi, in Ashtaroth's Lackey.*

THE LADY OF ALL OUR DREAMS

"Our distinguished alumnus," after being duly presented as such, had with vivacity delivered much the usual sort of Commencement Address. Yet John Charteris was in reality a trifle fagged.

The afternoon train had been vexatiously late. The little novelist had found it tedious to interchange inanities with the committee awaiting him at the Pullman steps. Nor had it amused him to huddle into evening-dress, and hasten through a perfunctory supper in order to reassure his audience at half-past eight precisely as to the unmitigated delight of which he was now conscious.

Nevertheless, he alluded with enthusiasm to the arena of life, to the dependence of America's destiny upon the younger generation, to the enviable part King's College had without exception played in history, and he depicted to Fairhaven the many glories of Fairhaven--past, present and approaching--in superlatives that would hardly have seemed inadequate if applied to Paradise. His oration, in short, was of a piece with the amiable bombast that the college students and Fairhaven at large were accustomed to applaud at every Finals--the sort of linguistic debauch that John Charteris himself remembered to have applauded as an undergraduate more years ago than he cared to acknowledge.

Pauline Romeyne had sat beside him then--yonder, upon the fourth bench from the front, where now another boy with painstakingly plastered hair was clapping hands. There was a girl on the right of this boy, too. There naturally would be. Mr. Charteris as he sat down was wondering if Pauline was within reach of his voice? and if she were, what was her surname nowadays?

Then presently the exercises were concluded, and the released auditors arose with an outwelling noise of multitudinous chatter, of shuffling feet, of rustling programs. Many of Mr. Charteris' audience, though, were contending against the general human outflow and pushing toward the platform, for Fairhaven was proud of John Charteris now that his colorful tales had risen, from the semi-oblivion of being cherished merely by people who cared seriously for beautiful things, to the distinction of being purchasable in railway stations; so that, in consequence, Fairhaven wished both to congratulate him and to renew acquaintanceship.

He, standing there, alert and quizzical, found it odd to note how unfamiliar beaming faces climbed out of the hurly-burly of retreating backs, to say, "Don't you remember me? I'm so-and-so." These were the people whom he had lived among once, and some of these had once been people whom he loved. Now there was hardly any one whom at a glance he would have recognized.

Nobody guessed as much. He was adjudged to be delightful, cordial, "and not a bit stuck-up, not spoiled at all, you know." To appear this was the talisman with which he banteringly encountered the universe.

But John Charteris, as has been said, was in reality a trifle fagged. When everybody had removed to the Gymnasium, where the dancing was to be, and he had been delightful there, too, for a whole half-hour, he grasped with avidity at his first chance to slip away, and did so under cover of a riotous two-step.

He went out upon the Campus.

He found this lawn untenanted, unless you chose to count the marble figure of Lord Penniston, made aerial and fantastic by the moonlight, standing as it it were on guard over the College. Mr. Charteris chose to count him. Whimsically, Mr. Charteris reflected that this battered nobleman's was the one familiar face he had exhumed in all Fairhaven. And what a deal of mirth and folly, too, the old fellow must have witnessed during his two hundred and odd years of sentry-duty! On warm, clear nights like this, in particular, when by ordinary there were only couples on the Campus, each couple discreetly remote from any of the others. Then Penniston would be aware of most portentous pauses (which a delectable and lazy conference of leaves made eloquent) because of many unfinished sentences. "Oh, YOU know what I mean, dear!" one would say as a last resort. And she-why, bless her heart! of course, she always did. . . . Heigho, youth's was a pleasant lunacy. . . .

Thus Charteris reflected, growing drowsy. She said, "You spoke very well tonight. Is it too late for congratulations?"

Turning, Mr. Charteris remarked, "As you are perfectly aware, all that I vented was just a deal of skimble-scamble stuff, a verbal syllabub of balderdash. No, upon reflection, I think I should rather describe it as a conglomeration of piffle, patriotism and pyrotechnics. Well, Madam Do-as-you-would-be-done-by, what would you have? You must give people what they want."

It was characteristic that he faced Pauline Romeyne--or was it still Romeyne? he wondered--precisely as if it had been fifteen minutes, rather than as many years, since they had last spoken together.

"Must one?" she asked. "Oh, yes, I know you have always thought that, but I do not quite see the necessity of it."

She sat upon the bench beside Lord Penniston's square marble pedestal. "And all the while you spoke I was thinking of those Saturday nights when your name was up for an oration or a debate before the Eclectics, and you would stay away and pay the fine rather than brave an audience."

"The tooth of Time," he reminded her, "has since then written wrinkles on my azure brow. The years slip away fugacious, and Time that brings forth her children only to devour them grins most hellishly, for Time changes all things and cultivates even in herself an appreciation of irony,--and, therefore, why shouldn't I have changed a trifle? You wouldn't have me put on exhibition as a *lusus naturae*?"

"Oh, but I wish you had not altered so entirely!" Pauline sighed.

"At least, you haven't," he declared. "Of course, I would be compelled to say so, anyhow. But in this happy instance courtesy and veracity come skipping arm-in-arm from my elated lips." And, indeed, it seemed to him that Pauline was marvelously little altered. "I wonder now," he said, and cocked his head, "I wonder now whose wife I am talking to?"

"No, Jack, I never married," she said quietly.

"It is selfish of me," he said, in the same tone, "but I am glad of that."

And so they sat a while, each thinking.

"I wonder," said Pauline, with that small plaintive voice which Charteris so poignantly remembered, "whether it is always like this? Oh, do the Overlords of Life and Death ALWAYS provide some obstacle to prevent what all of us have known in youth was possible from ever coming true?"

And again there was a pause which a delectable and lazy conference of leaves made eloquent.

"I suppose it is because they know that if it ever did come true, we would be gods like them." The ordinary associates of John Charteris, most certainly, would not have suspected him to be the speaker. "So they contrive the obstacle, or else they send false dreams--out of the gates of horn--and make the path smooth, very smooth, so that two dreamers may not be hindered on their way to the divorce-courts."

"Yes, they are jealous gods! oh, and ironical gods also! They grant the Dream, and chuckle while they grant it, I think, because they know that later they will be bringing their playthings face to face--each married, fat, inclined to optimism, very careful of decorum, and perfectly indifferent to each other. And then they get their fore-planned mirth, these Overlords of Life and Death. 'We gave you,' they chuckle, 'the loveliest and greatest thing infinity contains. And you bartered it because of a clerkship or a lying maxim or perhaps a finger-ring.' I suppose that they must laugh a great deal."

"Eh, what? But then you never married?" For masculinity in argument starts with the word it has found distasteful.

"Why, no."

"Nor I." And his tone implied that the two facts conjoined proved much.

"Miss Willoughby----?" she inquired.

Now, how in heaven's name, could a cloistered Fairhaven have surmised his intention of proposing on the first convenient opportunity to handsome, well-to-do Anne Willoughby? He shrugged his wonder off. "Oh, people will talk, you know. Let any man once find a woman has a tongue in her head, and the stage-direction is always 'Enter Rumor, painted full of tongues.'"

Pauline did not appear to have remarked his protest. "Yes,--in the end you will marry her. And her money will help, just as you have contrived to make every-thing else help, toward making John Charteris comfortable. She is not very clever, but she will always worship you, and so you two will not prove uncongenial. That is your real tragedy, if I could make you comprehend."

"So I am going to develop into a pig," he said, with relish,--"a lovable, con-tented, unambitious porcine, who is alike indifferent to the Tariff, the importance of Equal Suffrage and the market-price of hams, for all that he really cares about is to have his sty as comfortable as may be possible. That is exactly what I am going to develop into,--now, isn't it?" And John Charteris, sitting, as was his habitual fashion, with one foot tucked under him, laughed cheerily. Oh, just to be alive (he thought) was ample cause for rejoicing! and how deliciously her eyes, alert with slumbering fires, were peering through the moon-made shadows of her brows!

"Well----! something of the sort." Pauline was smiling, but restrainedly, and much as a woman does in condoning the naughtiness of her child. "And, oh, if only----"

"Why, precisely. 'If only!' quotha. Why, there you word the key-note, you touch the cornerstone, you ruthlessly illuminate the mainspring, of an intractable unfeeling universe. For instance, if only

> You were the Empress of Ayre and Skye,
> And I were Ahkond of Kong,
> We could dine every day on apple-pie,
> And peddle potatoes, and sleep in a sty,
> And people would say when we came to die,
> 'They *never* did anything wrong.'

But, as it is, our epitaphs will probably be nothing of the sort. So that there lurks, you see, much virtue in this 'if only.'"

Impervious to nonsense, she asked, "And have I not earned the right to lament that you are changed?"

"I haven't robbed more than six churches up to date," he grumbled. "What would you have?"

The answer came, downright, and, as he knew, entirely truthful: "I would have had you do all that you might have done."

But he must needs refine. "Why, no--you would have made me do it, wrung out the last drop. You would have bullied me and shamed me into being all that I might have been. I see that now." He spoke as if in wonder, with quickening speech. "Pauline, I haven't been entirely not worth while. Oh, yes, I know! I know I haven't written five-act tragedies which would be immortal, as you probably expected me to do. My books are not quite the books I was to write when you and I were young. But I have made at worst some neat, precise and joyous little tales which prevaricate tenderly about the universe and veil the pettiness of human nature with screens of verbal jewelwork. It is not the actual world they tell about, but a vastly superior place where the Dream is realized and everything which in youth we knew was possible comes true. It is a world we have all glimpsed, just once, and have not ever entered, and have not ever forgotten. So people like my little tales. . . . Do they induce delusions? Oh, well, you must give people what they want, and literature is a vast bazaar where customers come to purchase everything except mirrors."

She said soberly, "You need not make a jest of it. It is not ridiculous that you write of beautiful and joyous things because there was a time when living was really all one wonderful adventure, and you remember it."

"But, oh, my dear, my dear! such glum discussions are so sadly out-of-place on such a night as this," he lamented. "For it is a night of pearl-like radiancies and velvet shadows and delicate odors and big friendly stars that promise not to gossip, whatever happens. It is a night that hungers, and all its undistinguishable little sounds are voicing the night's hunger for masks and mandolins, for rope-ladders and balconies and serenades. It is a night . . . a night wherein I gratefully remember so many beautiful sad things that never happened . . . to John Charteris, yet surely happened once upon a time to me . . ."

"I think that I know what it is to remember--better than you do, Jack. But what do you remember?"

"In faith, my dear, the most Bedlamitish occurrences! It is a night that breeds deplorable insanities, I warn you. For I seem to remember how I sat somewhere, under a peach-tree, in clear autumn weather, and was content; but the importance had all gone out of things; and even you did not seem very important, hardly worth lying to, as I spoke lightly of my wasted love for you, half in hatred, and--yes, still half in adoration. For you were there, of course. And I remember how I came to you, in a sinister and brightly lighted place, where a horrible, staring frail old man lay dead at your feet; and you had murdered him; and heaven did not care, and we were old, and all our lives seemed just to end in futile tangle-work. And, again, I remember how we stood alone, with visible death crawling lazily toward us, as a big sullen sea rose higher and higher; and we little tinseled creatures waited, helpless, trapped and yearning. . . . There is a boat in that picture; I suppose it was deeply laden with pirates coming to slit our throats from ear to ear. I have forgotten that part, but I remember the tiny spot of courtplaster just above your painted lips. . . . Such are the jumbled pictures. They are bred of brain-fag, no doubt; yet, whatever be their lineage," said Charteris, happily, "they render glum discussion and platitudinous moralizing quite out of the question. So, let's pretend, Pauline, that we are not a bit more worldly-wise than those youngsters who are frisking yonder in the Gymnasium--for, upon my word, I dispute if we have ever done anything to suggest that we are. Don't let's be cowed a moment longer by those bits of paper with figures on them which our too-credulous fellow-idiots consider to be the only almanacs. Let's have back yesterday, let's tweak the nose of Time intrepidly." Then Charteris caroled:

"For Yesterday! for Yesterday!
I cry a reward for a Yesterday
Now lost or stolen or gone astray,
With all the laughter of Yesterday!"

"And how slight a loss was laughter," she murmured--still with the vague and gentle eyes of a day-dreamer--"as set against all that we never earned in youth, and so will never earn."

He inadequately answered "Bosh!" and later, "Do you remember----?" he began.

Yes, she remembered that, it developed. And "Do you remember----?" she in turn was asking later. It was to seem to him in retrospection that neither for the next half-hour began a sentence without this formula. It was as if they sought to use it as a master-word wherewith to reanimate the happinesses and sorrows of their common past, and as if they found the charm was potent to awaken the thin, powerless ghosts of emotions that were once despotic. For it was as if frail shadows and half-caught echoes were all they could evoke, it seemed to Charteris; and yet these shadows trooped with a wild grace, and the echoes thrilled him with the sweet and piercing surprise of a bird's call at midnight or of a bugle heard in prison.

Then twelve o'clock was heralded by the College bell, and Pauline arose as though this equable deep-throated interruption of the music's levity had been a signal. John Charteris saw her clearly now; and she was beautiful.

"I must go. You will not ever quite forget me, Jack. Such is my sorry comfort." It seemed to Charteris that she smiled as in mockery, and yet it was a very tender sort of derision. "Yes, you have made your books. You have done what you most desired to do. You have got all from life that you have asked of life. Oh, yes, you have got much from life. One prize, though, Jack, you missed."

He, too, had risen, quiet and perfectly sure of himself. "I haven't missed it. For you love me."

This widened her eyes. "Did I not always love you, Jack? Yes, even when you went away forever, and there were no letters, and the days were long. Yes, even knowing you, I loved you, John Charteris."

"Oh, I was wrong, all wrong," he cried; "and yet there is something to be said upon the other side, as always. . . ." Now Charteris was still for a while. The little man's chin was uplifted so that it was toward the stars he looked rather than at Pauline Romeyne, and when he spoke he seemed to meditate aloud. "I was born, I think, with the desire to make beautiful books--brave books that would preserve the glories of the Dream untarnished, and would re-create them for battered people, and re-awaken joy and magnanimity." Here he laughed, a little ruefully. "No, I do not think I can explain this obsession to any one who has never suffered from it. But I have never in my life permitted anything to stand in the way of my fulfilling this desire to serve the Dream by re-creating it for others with picked words, and that has cost me something. Yes, the Dream is an exacting master. My books, such as they are, have been made what they are at the dear price of never permitting myself to care seriously for anything else. I might not dare to dissipate my energies by taking any part in the drama I was attempting to re-write, because I must so jealously conserve all the force that was in me for the perfection of my lovelier version. That may not be the best way of making books, but it is the only one that was possible for me. I had so little natural talent, you see," said Charteris, wistfully, "and I was anxious to do so much with it. So I had always to be careful. It has been rather lonely, my dear. Now, looking back, it seems to me that the part I have played in all other people's lives has been the role of a tourist who enters a cafe chantant, a fortress, or a cathedral, with much the same forlorn sense of detachment, and observes what there is to see that may be worth remembering, and takes a note or two, perhaps, and then leaves the place forever. Yes, that is how I served the Dream and that is how I got my books. They are very beautiful books, I think, but they cost me fifteen years of human living and human intimacy, and they are hardly worth so much."

He turned to her, and his voice changed. "Oh, I was wrong, all wrong, and chance is kindlier than I deserve. For I have wandered after unprofitable gods, like a man blundering through a day of mist and fog, and I win home now in its golden sunset. I have laughed very much, my dear, but I was never happy until to-night. The Dream, as I now know, is not best served by making parodies of it, and it does not greatly matter after all whether a book be an epic or a directory. What really matters is that there is so much faith and love and kindliness which we can share with and provoke in others, and that by cleanly, simple, generous living we approach perfection in the highest and most lovely of all arts. . . . But you, I think, have always comprehended this. My dear, if I were worthy to kneel and kiss the dust you tread in I would do it. As it happens, I am not worthy. Pauline, there was a time when you and I were young together, when we aspired, when life passed as if it were to the measures of a noble music--a heart-wringing, an obdurate, an intolerable music, it might be, but always a lofty music. One strutted, no doubt--it was because one knew oneself to be indomitable. Eh, it is true I have won all I asked of life, very horribly true. All that I asked, poor fool! oh, I am weary of loneliness, and I know now that all the phantoms I have raised are only colorless shadows which belie the Dream, and they are hateful to me. I want just to recapture that old time we know of, and we two alone. I want to know the Dream again, Pauline,--the Dream which I had lost, had half forgotten, and have so pitifully parodied. I want to know the Dream again, Pauline, and you alone can help me."

"Oh, if I could! if even I could now, my dear!" Pauline Romeyne left him upon a sudden, crying this. And "So!" said Mr. Charteris.

He had been deeply shaken and very much in earnest; but he was never the man to give for any lengthy while too slack a rein to emotion; and so he now sat down upon the bench and lighted a cigarette and smiled. Yet he fully recognized himself to be the most enviable of men and an inhabitant of the most glorious world imaginable--a world wherein he very assuredly meant to marry Pauline Romeyne say, in the ensuing September. Yes, that would fit in well enough, although, of course, he would have to cancel the engagement to lecture in Milwaukee. . . . How lucky, too, it was that he had never actually committed himself with Anne Willoughby! for while money was an excellent thing to have, how infinitely less desirable it was to live perked up in golden sorrow than to feed flocks upon the Grampian Hills, where Freedom from the mountain height cried, "I go on forever, a prince can make a belted knight, and let who will be clever. . . ."

"--and besides, you'll catch your death of cold," lamented Rudolph Musgrave, who was now shaking Mr. Charteris' shoulder.

"Eh, what? Oh, yes, I daresay I was napping," the other mumbled. He stood and stretched himself luxuriously. "Well, anyhow, don't be such an unmitigated grandmother. You see, I have a bit of rather important business to attend to. Which way is Miss Romeyne?"

"Pauline Romeyne? why, but she married old General Ashmeade, you know. She was the gray-haired woman in purple who carried out her squalling brat when Taylor was introducing you, if you remember. She told me, while the General was getting the horses around, how sorry she was to miss your address, but they live three miles out, and Mrs. Ashmeade is simply a slave to the children. . . . Why, what in the world have you been dreaming about?"

"Eh, what? Oh, yes, I daresay I was only napping," Mr. Charteris observed. He was aware that within they were still playing a riotous two-step.

BALLAD OF PLAGIARY

"Freres et matres, vous qui cultivez"--PAUL VERVILLE.

Hey, my masters, lords and brothers, ye that till the fields of rhyme,
Are ye deaf ye will not hearken to the clamor of your time?

Still ye blot and change and polish--vary, heighten and transpose--
Old sonorous metres marching grandly to their tranquil close.

Ye have toiled and ye have fretted; ye attain perfected speech:
Ye have nothing new to utter and but platitudes to preach.

And your rhymes are all of loving, as within the old days when
Love was lord of the ascendant in the horoscopes of men.

Still ye make of love the utmost end and scope of all your art;
And, more blind than he you write of, note not what a modest part

Loving now may claim in living, when we have scant time to spare,
Who are plundering the sea-depths, taking tribute of the air,--

Whilst the sun makes pictures for us; since to-day, for good or ill,
Earth and sky and sea are harnessed, and the lightnings work our will.

Hey, my masters, all these love-songs by dust-hidden mouths were sung

That ye mimic and re-echo with an artful-artless tongue,--

Sung by poets close to nature, free to touch her garments' hem
Whom to-day ye know not truly; for ye only copy them.

Them ye copy--copy always, with your backs turned to the sun,
Caring not what man is doing, noting that which man has done.

We are talking over telephones, as Shakespeare could not talk;
We are riding out in motor-cars where Homer had to walk;

And pictures Dante labored on of mediaeval Hell
The nearest cinematograph paints quicker, and as well.

But ye copy, copy always;--and ye marvel when ye find
This new beauty, that new meaning,--while a model stands behind,

Waiting, young and fair as ever, till some singer turn and trace
Something of the deathless wonder of life lived in any place.

Hey, my masters, turn from piddling to the turmoil and the strife!
Cease from sonneting, my brothers; let us fashion songs from life.

Thus I wrote ere Percie passed me. . . . Then did I epitomize
All life's beauty in one poem, and make haste to eulogize
Quite the fairest thing life boasts of, for I wrote of Percie's eyes.

EXPLICIT DECAS POETARUM

www.bookjungle.com *email: sales@bookjungle.com fax: 630-214-0564 mail: Book Jungle PO Box 2226 Champaign, IL 61825*

The Codes Of Hammurabi And Moses
W. W. Davies

QTY

The discovery of the Hammurabi Code is one of the greatest achievements of archaeology, and is of paramount interest, not only to the student of the Bible, but also to all those interested in ancient history...

Religion   **ISBN:** *1-59462-338-4*   **Pages:132**
MSRP $12.95

The Theory of Moral Sentiments
Adam Smith

QTY

This work from 1749. contains original theories of conscience amd moral judgment and it is the foundation for systemof morals.

Philosophy   **ISBN:** *1-59462-777-0*   **Pages:536**
MSRP $19.95

Jessica's First Prayer
Hesba Stretton

QTY

In a screened and secluded corner of one of the many railway-bridges which span the streets of London there could be seen a few years ago, from five o'clock every morning until half past eight, a tidily set-out coffee-stall, consisting of a trestle and board, upon which stood two large tin cans, with a small fire of charcoal burning under each so as to keep the coffee boiling during the early hours of the morning when the work-people were thronging into the city on their way to their daily toil...

Childrens   **ISBN:** *1-59462-373-2*   **Pages:84**
MSRP $9.95

My Life and Work
Henry Ford

QTY

Henry Ford revolutionized the world with his implementation of mass production for the Model T automobile. Gain valuable business insight into his life and work with his own auto-biography... "We have only started on our development of our country we have not as yet, with all our talk of wonderful progress, done more than scratch the surface. The progress has been wonderful enough but..."

Biographies/   **ISBN:** *1-59462-198-5*   **Pages:300**
MSRP $21.95

The Art of Cross-Examination
Francis Wellman

QTY

I presume it is the experience of every author, after his first book is published upon an important subject, to be almost overwhelmed with a wealth of ideas and illustrations which could readily have been included in his book, and which to his own mind, at least, seem to make a second edition inevitable. Such certainly was the case with me; and when the first edition had reached its sixth impression in five months, I rejoiced to learn that it seemed to my publishers that the book had met with a sufficiently favorable reception to justify a second and considerably enlarged edition. ..

Pages:412

Reference　　ISBN: *1-59462-647-2*　　*MSRP $19.95*

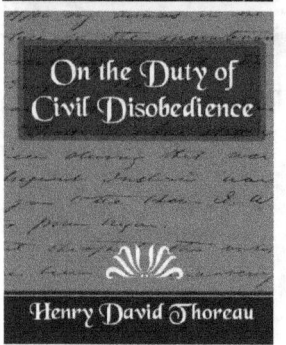

On the Duty of Civil Disobedience
Henry David Thoreau

QTY

Thoreau wrote his famous essay, On the Duty of Civil Disobedience, as a protest against an unjust but popular war and the immoral but popular institution of slave-owning. He did more than write—he declined to pay his taxes, and was hauled off to gaol in consequence. Who can say how much this refusal of his hastened the end of the war and of slavery ?

Law　　　ISBN: *1-59462-747-9*　　**Pages:48**

MSRP $7.45

Dream Psychology Psychoanalysis for Beginners
Sigmund Freud

QTY

Sigmund Freud, born Sigismund Schlomo Freud (May 6, 1856 - September 23, 1939), was a Jewish-Austrian neurologist and psychiatrist who co-founded the psychoanalytic school of psychology. Freud is best known for his theories of the unconscious mind, especially involving the mechanism of repression; his redefinition of sexual desire as mobile and directed towards a wide variety of objects; and his therapeutic techniques, especially his understanding of transference in the therapeutic relationship and the presumed value of dreams as sources of insight into unconscious desires.

Pages:196

Psychology　　ISBN: *1-59462-905-6*　　*MSRP $15.45*

The Miracle of Right Thought
Orison Swett Marden

QTY

Believe with all of your heart that you will do what you were made to do. When the mind has once formed the habit of holding cheerful, happy, prosperous pictures, it will not be easy to form the opposite habit. It does not matter how improbable or how far away this realization may see, or how dark the prospects may be, if we visualize them as best we can, as vividly as possible, hold tenaciously to them and vigorously struggle to attain them, they will gradually become actualized, realized in the life. But a desire, a longing without endeavor, a yearning abandoned or held indifferently will vanish without realization.

Pages:360

Self Help　　　ISBN: *1-59462-644-8*　　*MSRP $25.45*

QTY

The Rosicrucian Cosmo-Conception Mystic Christianity *by Max Heindel*   ISBN: *1-59462-188-8* **$38.95**
The Rosicrucian Cosmo-conception is not dogmatic, neither does it appeal to any other authority than the reason of the student. It is: not controversial, but is: sent forth in the, hope that it may help to clear...   New Age/Religion Pages 646

Abandonment To Divine Providence *by Jean-Pierre de Caussade*   ISBN: *1-59462-228-0* **$25.95**
"The Rev. Jean Pierre de Caussade was one of the most remarkable spiritual writers of the Society of Jesus in France in the 18th Century. His death took place at Toulouse in 1751. His works have gone through many editions and have been republished...   Inspirational/Religion Pages 400

Mental Chemistry *by Charles Haanel*   ISBN: *1-59462-192-6* **$23.95**
Mental Chemistry allows the change of material conditions by combining and appropriately utilizing the power of the mind. Much like applied chemistry creates something new and unique out of careful combinations of chemicals the mastery of mental chemistry...   New Age Pages 354

The Letters of Robert Browning and Elizabeth Barret Barrett 1845-1846 vol II   ISBN: *1-59462-193-4* **$35.95**
by Robert Browning and Elizabeth Barrett   Biographies Pages 596

Gleanings In Genesis (volume I) *by Arthur W. Pink*   ISBN: *1-59462-130-6* **$27.45**
Appropriately has Genesis been termed "the seed plot of the Bible" for in it we have, in germ form, almost all of the great doctrines which are afterwards fully developed in the books of Scripture which follow...   Religion/Inspirational Pages 420

The Master Key *by L. W. de Laurence*   ISBN: *1-59462-001-6* **$30.95**
In no branch of human knowledge has there been a more lively increase of the spirit of research during the past few years than in the study of Psychology, Concentration and Mental Discipline. The requests for authentic lessons in Thought Control, Mental Discipline and...   New Age/Business Pages 422

The Lesser Key Of Solomon Goetia *by L. W. de Laurence*   ISBN: *1-59462-092-X* **$9.95**
This translation of the first book of the "Lernegton" which is now for the first time made accessible to students of Talismanic Magic was done, after careful collation and edition, from numerous Ancient Manuscripts in Hebrew, Latin, and French...   New Age/Occult Pages 92

Rubaiyat Of Omar Khayyam *by Edward Fitzgerald*   ISBN: *1-59462-332-5* **$13.95**
Edward Fitzgerald, whom the world has already learned, in spite of his own efforts to remain within the shadow of anonymity, to look upon as one of the rarest poets of the century, was born at Bredfield, in Suffolk, on the 31st of March, 1809. He was the third son of John Purcell...   Music Pages 172

Ancient Law *by Henry Maine*   ISBN: *1-59462-128-4* **$29.95**
The chief object of the following pages is to indicate some of the earliest ideas of mankind, as they are reflected in Ancient Law, and to point out the relation of those ideas to modern thought.   Religiom/History Pages 452

Far-Away Stories *by William J. Locke*   ISBN: *1-59462-129-2* **$19.45**
"Good wine needs no bush, but a collection of mixed vintages does. And this book is just such a collection. Some of the stories I do not want to remain buried for ever in the museum files of dead magazine-numbers an author's not unpardonable vanity..."   Fiction Pages 272

Life of David Crockett *by David Crockett*   ISBN: *1-59462-250-7* **$27.45**
"Colonel David Crockett was one of the most remarkable men of the times in which he lived. Born in humble life, but gifted with a strong will, an indomitable courage, and unremitting perseverance...   Biographies/New Age Pages 424

Lip-Reading *by Edward Nitchie*   ISBN: *1-59462-206-X* **$25.95**
Edward B. Nitchie, founder of the New York School for the Hard of Hearing, now the Nitchie School of Lip-Reading, Inc, wrote "LIP-READING Principles and Practice". The development and perfecting of this meritorious work on lip-reading was an undertaking...   How-to Pages 400

A Handbook of Suggestive Therapeutics, Applied Hypnotism, Psychic Science   ISBN: *1-59462-214-0* **$24.95**
by Henry Munro   Health/New Age/Health/Self-help Pages 376

A Doll's House: and Two Other Plays *by Henrik Ibsen*   ISBN: *1-59462-112-8* **$19.95**
Henrik Ibsen created this classic when in revolutionary 1848 Rome. Introducing some striking concepts in playwriting for the realist genre, this play has been studied the world over.   Fiction/Classics/Plays 308

The Light of Asia *by sir Edwin Arnold*   ISBN: *1-59462-204-3* **$13.95**
In this poetic masterpiece, Edwin Arnold describes the life and teachings of Buddha. The man who was to become known as Buddha to the world was born as Prince Gautama of India but he rejected the worldly riches and abandoned the reigns of power when...   Religion/History/Biographies Pages 170

The Complete Works of Guy de Maupassant *by Guy de Maupassant*   ISBN: *1-59462-157-8* **$16.95**
"For days and days, nights and nights, I had dreamed of that first kiss which was to consecrate our engagement, and I knew not on what spot I should put my lips..."   Fiction/Classics Pages 240

The Art of Cross-Examination *by Francis L. Wellman*   ISBN: *1-59462-309-0* **$26.95**
Written by a renowned trial lawyer, Wellman imparts his experience and uses case studies to explain how to use psychology to extract desired information through questioning.   How-to/Science/Reference Pages 408

Answered or Unanswered? *by Louisa Vaughan*   ISBN: *1-59462-248-5* **$10.95**
Miracles of Faith in China   Religion Pages 112

The Edinburgh Lectures on Mental Science (1909) *by Thomas*   ISBN: *1-59462-008-3* **$11.95**
This book contains the substance of a course of lectures recently given by the writer in the Queen Street Hall, Edinburgh. Its purpose is to indicate the Natural Principles governing the relation between Mental Action and Material Conditions...   New Age/Psychology Pages 148

Ayesha *by H. Rider Haggard*   ISBN: *1-59462-301-5* **$24.95**
Verily and indeed it is the unexpected that happens! Probably if there was one person upon the earth from whom the Editor of this, and of a certain previous history, did not expect to hear again...   Classics Pages 380

Ayala's Angel *by Anthony Trollope*   ISBN: *1-59462-352-X* **$29.95**
The two girls were both pretty, but Lucy who was twenty-one who supposed to be simple and comparatively unattractive, whereas Ayala was credited, as her Bombwhat romantic name might show, with poetic charm and a taste for romance. Ayala when her father died was nineteen...   Fiction Pages 484

The American Commonwealth *by James Bryce*   ISBN: *1-59462-286-8* **$34.45**
An interpretation of American democratic political theory. It examines political mechanics and society from the perspective of Scotsman James Bryce   Politics Pages 572

Stories of the Pilgrims *by Margaret P. Pumphrey*   ISBN: *1-59462-116-0* **$17.95**
This book explores pilgrims religious oppression in England as well as their escape to Holland and eventual crossing to America on the Mayflower, and their early days in New England...   History Pages 268

QTY

The Fasting Cure *by Sinclair Upton*   ISBN: *1-59462-222-1*   **$13.95**
*In the Cosmopolitan Magazine for May, 1910, and in the Contemporary Review (London) for April, 1910, I published an article dealing with my experi-
ences in fasting. I have written a great many magazine articles, but never one which attracted so much attention...* New Age/Self Help/Health Pages 164

Hebrew Astrology *by Sepharial*   ISBN: *1-59462-308-2*   **$13.45**
*In these days of advanced thinking it is a matter of common observation that we have left many of the old landmarks behind and that we are now pressing
forward to greater heights and to a wider horizon than that which represented the mind-content of our progenitors...* Astrology Pages 144

Thought Vibration or The Law of Attraction in the Thought World   ISBN: *1-59462-127-6*   **$12.95**

by William Walker Atkinson   Psychology/Religion Pages 144

Optimism *by Helen Keller*   ISBN: *1-59462-108-X*   **$15.95**
*Helen Keller was blind, deaf, and mute since 19 months old, yet famously learned how to overcome these handicaps, communicate with the world, and
spread her lectures promoting optimism. An inspiring read for everyone...* Biographies/Inspirational Pages 84

Sara Crewe *by Frances Burnett*   ISBN: *1-59462-360-0*   **$9.45**
*In the first place, Miss Minchin lived in London. Her home was a large, dull, tall one, in a large, dull square, where all the houses were alike, and all the
sparrows were alike, and where all the door-knockers made the same heavy sound...* Childrens/Classic Pages 88

The Autobiography of Benjamin Franklin *by Benjamin Franklin*   ISBN: *1-59462-135-7*   **$24.95**
*The Autobiography of Benjamin Franklin has probably been more extensively read than any other American historical work, and no other book of its kind
has had such ups and downs of fortune. Franklin lived for many years in England, where he was agent...* Biographies/History Pages 332

Name	
Email	
Telephone	
Address	
City, State ZIP	

☐ **Credit Card**   ☐ **Check / Money Order**

Credit Card Number	
Expiration Date	
Signature	

Please Mail to: Book Jungle
                     PO Box 2226
                     Champaign, IL 61825
or Fax to: 630-214-0564

ORDERING INFORMATION

web: *www.bookjungle.com*
email: *sales@bookjungle.com*
fax: *630-214-0564*
mail: *Book Jungle PO Box 2226 Champaign, IL 61825*
or PayPal *to sales@bookjungle.com*

Please contact us for bulk discounts

DIRECT-ORDER TERMS

**20% Discount if You Order
Two or More Books**
Free Domestic Shipping!
Accepted: Master Card, Visa,
Discover, American Express